LS
D1335087

Leabh
SCHOOLS LIB
Inv/96 : 3901   Price IR£3.99
Title: lantern moon
Class:

The
Lantern Moon

The
Lantern Moon

MAEVE FRIEL

BEACON BOOKS

POOLBEG

Published 1996
by Poolbeg Press Ltd
123 Baldoyle Industrial Estate
Dublin 13, Ireland

© Maeve Friel 1996

The moral right of the author has been asserted.

The Publishers gratefully acknowledge the support of
The Arts Council.

A catalogue record for this book is available from the British Library.

ISBN 1 85371 676 6

All rights reserved. No part of this publication may be reproduced or transmitted in any form or by any means, electronic or mechanical, including photography, recording, or any information storage or retrieval system, without permission in writing from the publisher. The book is sold subject to the condition that it shall not, by way of trade or otherwise, be lent, resold or otherwise circulated without the publisher's prior consent in any form of binding or cover other than that in which it is published and without a similar condition, including this condition, being imposed on the subsequent purchaser.

Cover illustration by Alex Callaway
Cover design by Poolbeg Group Services Ltd
Set by Poolbeg Group Services Ltd in Goudy 11.5/15
Printed by The Guernsey Press Ltd,
Vale, Guernsey, Channel Islands.

About the Author

❧

Maeve Friel was born in Derry, educated in Dublin, and currently lives in Ireland. Two of her books for children, *The Deerstone* and *Distant Voices*, were published to critical acclaim and shortlisted for the Bisto Book Award and the RAI (Reading Association of Ireland) Book Award. Maeve Friel writes for both children and adults.

Also by Maeve Friel

≈

The Deerstone
Charlie's Story
Distant Voices

Praise for *Distant Voices*

"Rarely in Irish children's writing has the time-slip theme been handled with such assurance."
Children's Books Ireland

"The general tone of displacement and unease suits the subject-matter and its environment, leaving the reader uneasy too."
The Irish Times

৺

Praise for *Charlie's Story*

"Friel's language and dialogue are not unlike Anne Fine's: they are loaded with character implications."
Children's Books Ireland

"Disturbing and compelling."
Sunday Independent

Acknowledgements

I am very grateful to Connie Brooks whose pamphlet on the glove-making industry in Ludlow and the children who worked for it inspired this book. And to Jill Howarth of the Silk Top Hat Gallery in Quality Square who kindly allowed me to read her research material on the top hat factory that once occupied her art gallery.

For PK

"White in the moon the long road lies,
The moon stands blank above;
White in the moon the long road lies
That leads me from my love."

A Shropshire Lad XXXVI, A E Housman

Chapter 1

For most of the journey from Plymouth, the road was barely passable. It was narrow, muddy and so full of potholes and ruts that the carriages were frequently stuck fast in the muck. Twice, two of the horses broke their harnesses trying to break free and, once, a wheel came off one of the luggage waggons at the rear, sending the prince's belongings careering down to the bottom of the hill. They had made three overnight stops at inns along the way, in Exeter, Bath and Gloucester. Everywhere large crowds came out to wave or stare as they passed by. The whole of England was curious to see "Bony's brother": after all, the country had been at war with Napoleon Bonaparte for years and years.

William Spears had been sent down by Lord Powis to act as look-out. He had been sitting with his feet dangling over the edge of Ludford Bridge since first light. It was so cold that he felt his backside must have frozen to the stone bridge. His hands had long since lost all feeling no matter how hard he pressed them under his armpits. His nose dripped. His ears under his new black top hat smarted with pain. His empty tummy rumbled. At last, above the hypnotic sound of the floodwater pouring over the weirs, he heard the distant rumble of carriage wheels and the snorting of the horses as they reached their home stretch.

A moment or two later, the first coach appeared around the corner, and the coachman, bleary-eyed and spattered from head to toe in black mud, raised his horn to his lips and sounded three short blasts to let the travellers know they had arrived at Ludlow. Dinner at last, thought William, racing off through the lanes on rather stiff legs to tell Lord Powis that Lucien Bonaparte, the new tenant of Dinham House, had finally arrived in town, and to claim the two pence he had been promised.

The eight carriages, each drawn by four grey horses, crossed the river Teme at a cracking pace, passed the woollen mill, went through the narrow gate in the walls and climbed the steep hill of Broad Street into the town. At the summit, they turned sharp left, and entered the market square, setting every cock and hen squawking in their cages and every dog barking and running along at their wheels. This only encouraged the coachmen to drive faster: they cracked their whips, scattering the dogs away in all directions with their tails between their legs. The men and women at the market stalls had scarcely had time to look up from their business and turn their astonished faces towards the extraordinary parade than the coaches had skirted the square, followed the road round by the stark grey ruins of the castle, and pulled in to the driveway of Dinham House, where the arrival of so many coaches all at once cast dark shadows into the basement kitchen and set Mrs Stringer, the housekeeper, into a tizzy.

"The Lord preserve us, it's Lucien Bonaparte here already," she cried, coming up the kitchen stairs as fast as her short chubby legs could carry her. She patted her hair into place at the hall mirror and looked out the tall windows. Lord Powis was already standing there, helping the prince and his party down from their carriages. There seemed to be far more people than she had been told to expect. "Here in Ludlow," she gasped, "and the meat scarcely ten minutes in the oven. Annie Spears," she shouted, "where are you, girl? Have you set the fires yet?"

Annie Spears, the parlour-maid, came running out into the hall. She was quite red-faced for she had been admiring herself and her new uniform in the parlour mirror. She had never seen a full-length reflection of herself before and was secretly pleased with what she saw.

"No, ma'am, I can't," she replied, breathlessly. "Sam, I mean Samuel Price, is still up the chimney."

"That boy!" declared Mrs Stringer. "I'll swing for him."

"I've been telling him, ma'am, to get a move on, but he says he can't work any faster."

"We'll see about that." She pushed past Annie and strode into the drawing-room. Kneeling down in front of the hearth, she shouted up the chimney.

"Samuel Price, do you hear me?"

There was a muffled response.

"If you don't get down here this instant, I'll light the fire in the grate and see how you like it up there then."

Samuel Price was perched on a dark ledge high up beyond the first floor. His elbows and knees were streaming blood from pushing himself up the long twisting soot-covered flues of the chimney and his eyes and mouth were so full of smuts and soot that he could neither see nor speak. His lungs had given out and he just needed a few more minutes to catch his breath before beginning the long painful descent back into the drawing-room.

"Chimney-boy? Do you hear me? I'm counting to ten. One, two, three . . ."

There was a distant thump, and then a scraping sound that reminded Annie of the rats which she heard scratching in the yard behind the tanners' cottages where she lived. A light sprinkling of soot fell down into the grate. A moment or two later, the bare feet, the ragged trousers and finally the black face of Samuel Price appeared panting but smiling in the hearth.

"What's your hurry then, ma'am? That's the last one done and it's not even dinner time."

"I'll give you dinner," snapped Mrs Stringer, sarcastically. "Don't you know the prince Bonaparte has just driven up and will be looking to come in here directly."

"Bonaparte? You mean Napoleon, our mortal enemy, what Admiral Nelson and the whole of the British navy have been trying to beat all these years? Napoleon? Here in Ludlow?"

"No! Not Napoleon!" Mrs Stringer was in no mood for explanations. She grabbed Sam by the shoulder and dragged him out. "Come out of that grate, you silly boy. Where's your master got to then? He's not up the chimney too, is he?"

"Master Bessell up the chimney? Not on your life. He's round the Angel Inn, more than likely."

Mrs Stringer hauled herself to her feet and steadied herself against the mantelpiece. The boy looked in a bad way, wheezing dreadfully.

"Spears, take that boy to the kitchen and give him some bread. Then get yourself back to work. Not that way," she shouted as Samuel nipped across the wooden floor leaving a trail of black prints behind him. "The back stairs, if you please – and mind you don't touch anything."

Annie led Samuel down to the basement. The kitchens were a flurry of activity with more people than Annie had ever seen working there. A man was uncorking bottles of wine and laying them out on a tray with glasses, the cook was slicing up a huge yellow cake studded with red cherries, and the maids were bobbing up and down in front of her as they carried off tray after tray of food and refreshments for the new arrivals.

"Who brought that dirty boy in to my good clean kitchen?" scowled the cook as soon as she spotted Annie and Samuel standing by the door.

"I did," said Annie, her voice hardly more than a whisper. "Mrs Stringer says he's to have some bread, if you please, ma'am."

"Not before he's washed hisself. I won't have hands like that touching the food in my kitchen. What's your name, chimney boy?"

"Samuel Price, ma'am, Sam to those that know me."

"Well, Samuel Price, you wash your face and hands out there at the back and then Spears here will give you something to eat."

There was a well in one of the sculleries off the main kitchen. Annie pumped up a bucket of cold water which Sam dabbed uselessly at his sooty blood-streaked knees.

"Are they sore?" asked Annie.

"Not half," said Sam.

"You need hot water with plenty salt in it to scrub that dirt off," said a voice. It was Arthur, one of the footmen, on his way past with a huge wooden carriage-box balanced on his shoulders. "And to toughen up the skin. Wait there."

In a few moments he was back with a basin of almost boiling hot salt water and began to clean Sam's bleeding knees and feet. Tears sprang to Sam's eyes as the salt stung the open flesh. "You must bear it, Sam, or else those kneecaps will never harden up. What you really ought to do is stand in front of the fire and let the salt dry. You want skin like an elephant's hide to do your job. Doesn't your master tell you that? Who do you work for anyway?"

"Master Bessell from the High Street, sir."

"That drunkard," Arthur swore under his breath. "I worked for him myself when I was your age."

"You were a chimney sweep?" Annie and Sam stared

6

at Arthur in all his finery, his embroidered waist-coat, his tails, his neat yellow hair, his tiny pointed leather shoes. "For three long years. I ran away once and hid in the shepherd's hut above Whitcliffe till they found me. But luckily enough, I was getting too big to climb by then, and Bessell let me go before the soot killed me off. Do you have to do it, Sam? Why don't you go to school? This sweeping is going to do you in."

"I went to school for a week once with Mr D'arcy – that's how I know to write my name," said Sam proudly. "And I wasn't always a sweep – I used to be a bird-scarer when I lived in the country. I liked that, sitting on the fence shouting at the crows and the jackdaws to stop them eating the seeds." He sniffed at the smell of roasting meat wafting in from the kitchen. "But working in houses is better. That way I get more food. Usually."

"Right," said Arthur, smiling. He wrung out the dish-rag and wiped away the last of the dirt from Sam's face. "The chimney sweep wants his grub. If you stay here nice and quiet, Sam, this girl here will bring you in as great a feast as ever you've seen. What's your name, girl?"

"Annie Spears, if you please," whispered Annie. *Please let him not know my father*, she thought to herself.

"Are you new here, Annie?"

"Yes, I just started yesterday." Annie smiled and smoothed down the front of her new black dress. "They needed more help because of the French prince."

"Are you anything to William Spears that works in the silk top hat factory?"

"He's my brother," said Annie, blushing. *He knows who we are.*

Arthur smiled. "What age are you, then?"

"Eleven."

"So this is your first job?"

Annie shook her head. "I used to sew gloves."

"Well then, you know what hard work is," said Arthur. "Just do what you're told here at Dinham. Keep out from under Mrs Stringer's feet and you'll be all right. Her bark is worse than her bite in any case. Come to me if you need anything." He winked, swung the trunk he had been carrying back up on to his shoulder and swayed off down the corridor. "Follow me, Annie Spears, and we'll get Sam some food."

Sam settled down to wait beside the dripping pump. Above his head, through the narrow basement windows, he could see the legs of the horses and the wheels of the carriages. Pink and gold stockinged footmen passed back and forth lugging trunks, hat boxes, carriage boxes, bird cages, even oddly-shaped cases that might have held musical instruments, up the stairs to the front door. Foreign voices called out to one another. Sam leant his back against the stone surround of the well and closed his eyes. He had been working up the chimneys for the best part of seven hours without a break.

As soon as Annie reappeared in the kitchen, Mrs Stringer grabbed her by the back of her skirt, thrust a huge tray groaning with tea things into her arms and propelled her towards the stairs.

"You, girl, where have you been? Take this tray up to

the French maids. They're in the music room with the children."

"But. . ." began Annie.

"And stop dawdling," she shouted, as Annie picked her way uncertainly up the uneven stone steps, staggering under the weight of the tray. "There's no work in this house for idlers."

"What about Sam and his dinner?" Annie thought but knew better than to say anything.

In the hall, her way was barred by two gentlemen standing talking at the foot of the staircase. She recognised the taller one, Lord Powis, the owner of Dinham House, for she had sometimes seen him walking with his dogs on Whitcliffe Common. The other man was small and dark-eyed with curly side-whiskers and a great shock of black hair above one of the highest foreheads Annie had ever seen. He was very handsome and knew it for he kept stealing glances at himself in the long hall mirror. His clothes were dazzling compared to Lord Powis' black suit. He wore a silk coat with tails, a blue velvet waistcoat, sprinkled with tiny oak leaves, dark green knickerbockers, white stockings, and huge lace ruffles at his neck and wrists. Annie had never seen such a dandy. She curtseyed, a quick bob for her knees were already almost buckling under her heavy burden, but the men did not even notice she was there and kept on talking.

"Of course we shall have a larger house ready for you as soon as possible," Lord Powis was explaining, "but, in the meantime, I hope you and your good wife, lady

Alexandrine, will be comfortable here. If there is anything I can do to make your stay a pleasant one . . . to be honest, we were not informed your party was so great in number."

"Under the circumstances, my Lord, we shall try to make ourselves comfortable," replied Lucien Bonaparte, in his strange attractive accent. "There are not so many of us, you know, just thirty-two. My dear wife, the children and their tutor, my physician, the chaplain, a few servants. Not so many." He shrugged and spread his hands open. "You know, of course, Lord Powis, that your government has forbidden us to travel outside the town."

"Yes, indeed, but you must not think of yourselves as prisoners. I think you will find society in Ludlow very agreeable. It is a small town but handsome to look at, with many pretty walks around the river and the castle, and there are Assemblies each week, and concerts, and theatre, and of course the summer races, too, to look forward to."

"No doubt," said Lucien Bonaparte, thoughtfully, "but how will the local society react to the presence of a Bonaparte while England is at war with France?"

Lord Powis pursed his lips. "They know or they soon will know that you are no friend of your brother, Napoleon. I am sure you will have no cause for complaint. On the contrary, the town will welcome you and your family with open arms."

Annie could bear the weight of the tray no longer. Her fingers gripping the handles were turning to jelly and she was afraid she would drop the whole thing if she could not set it down at once. "Don't speak unless you're spoken to, mind," Mrs Stringer had drummed into her over and over the day before when she had come to take up her new job. Annie coughed. The cups rattled.

The French prince turned at last and saw her.

"Ah, such a tiny person and such an immense assortment of cups. Allow me, little one," and he pushed open the double doors for Annie to enter the room. Annie stumbled forward, her cheeks burning with embarrassment.

To her surprise, the room was empty. Her first thought was that she had come to the wrong place for she still didn't really know her way around the huge house. She laid down her tray on the table in front of the white marble fire-place and looked around. It was a long room, with high windows facing out on to the gardens at the front and side of the house. The ceilings and walls were decorated with plaster motifs of viols and flutes, harps and other musical instruments. It had to be the music room, just like Mrs Stringer had said. She gazed up at a fat cherub playing a lute, and a choir of angels with round open mouths, wondering what to do next. Should she carry the tray back to the kitchen, leave it where it was, or take it with her while she hunted for the French maids? The sound of voices at the door made her jump. For a moment she thought of hiding behind the velvet curtains but waited too long. She froze as the double doors opened once more and in came, not the maids, but Lucien's wife, Alexandrine, and the Bonaparte children, all chattering and laughing.

There were two very little ones, a boy of about two and a girl of three each holding their mother by the hand, then two more, another boy and girl, both about seven or eight. Behind them came three older girls, the smallest about the same age as Annie herself, but dressed like an angel. Her dress, bright scarlet silk shot through with threads of gold, glittered in the light of the log fire. Annie thought she had never seen anyone so beautiful.

"Parlez-vous français?" the mother asked Annie.

Annie looked at her with wide horrified eyes.

"Non? it doesn't matter." She picked up the smallest little boy and absent-mindedly stroked his head while, with the other hand, she held out biscuits to the other children. "Will you pour out some tea?" she said to Annie. "I am quite exhausted from the coach journey. Charlotte, my dear, call my maid. Christine-Egypta, come and take Paul-Marie."

Christine-Egypta, the girl in the scarlet dress, moved across the room as if sliding on castors beneath her long skirts. She lifted the baby from her mother's lap and set him down on a rug in front of the fire. Watching her graceful movements, Annie felt ashamed, ashamed of her scrubbed red hands jerkily pouring out the tea, ashamed of her stiff creaking apron and her starched collar which had been digging into her neck all day. It had already left a nasty red weal like a ring of scorched skin. She wanted to be downstairs in the kitchen, safe among people she knew, people who spoke like her. No, more than anything, she wanted to be back home in Corve Street with her mother and Libby.

She was waiting for Madame Bonaparte to dismiss her when there was a knock at the door and Arthur the footman entered. "Madame, Prince Lucien wishes to advise you there are visitors from the town who have called to pay their respects. Will you see Mr Leonard Evans?"

Annie's blood ran cold when she heard the name. She backed towards the recess of the window and stood, half-hidden behind the curtains. The baby, Paul-Marie, thinking she was playing hide-and-seek with him, chuckled and started to crawl towards her.

Lady Alexandrine laid down her china cup and raised her eyebrows as if at a loss to know why she should have to see people she did not know so soon after her arrival. She could hear her husband's voice outside. This situation with the English was so difficult. How was she to know if they were prisoners or guests of the nation?

"Thank you, young man. If my husband wishes, I shall be happy to see Mr Evans."

The visitor came in clutching a flat black box against his stomach. Mr Evans was a large round man on short bow-legs so that when he moved he swayed like a dancing bear. He advanced into the room, bowing from the waist, which placed such a strain on his waistcoat buttons that one popped off and sprang across the room in front of him. He seemed put out by the sight of so many children.

He took Alexandrine's small white hand in his podgy one and kissed it, then, worried that perhaps that was not quite "the done thing" placed it abruptly back on her lap.

"Leonard Evans, at your service, Madame. Master Glover of Ludlow. With your permission?" He laid his handsome black lacquer box carefully on a side-table and bent down to undo the gold catch. Annie bit her lip. She shrank back further into the window recess, terrified he would recognise her and say something. The young princes and princesses gathered around the table to see what his box contained.

The box was full of gloves, gloves of every size and variety and colour. There were gloves made of the finest kid leathers, silk gloves and satin gloves, ones all done up with ribbon and lace, velvet gloves with tiny pearl buttons that buttoned right up to the elbows, gloves that would have been perfect for balls and dances, others trimmed with white rabbit fur for the coldest winter days. All the young princes and princesses began to seize them, pulling them from their orderly rows in the beautiful box, chattering and exclaiming in their strange language while Mr Evans looked on with mounting alarm. "Dear me," he said, frowning and smiling at the same time, as he smoothed the discarded gloves and hunted on the table for matching pairs. His face, which was always a little purplish, had become quite red.

"It would be a great honour, Your Royal Highnesses, if you would accept these gifts from the Guild of Glovers of Ludlow. The town is renowned for the quality of its gloves," he said, swelling slightly. "We are honoured to have a family of such distinction here and hope we may be of service to you . . ."

Alexandrine withdrew the tiniest pair of soft white

leather gloves from the box and held them out towards her daughters admiringly.

"Look, they are scarcely big enough for the baby, for Paul-Marie."

"How sweet they are," said Christine-Egypta. "Let me see if they fit him." She glided over to the window where the little boy had now plopped down at Annie's feet and was busily inspecting his toes.

"Come on, bébé," she said, giving Annie a dazzling smile, as she scooped the baby up in her arms and carried him back to his mother. The children gathered around as Alexandrine pulled the tiny gloves on to the boy's small plump hands.

"Oh, monsieur Evans, they are divine. They could have been made especially for him. Look, Christine-Egypta, Letitia, do you see how tiny the stitches are around the fingers, the little thumbs. Only a fairy, a small English fairy, could make such perfect stitches."

Annie Spears watched Leonard Evans' smirking face and felt sick. She thought of how she and her sister Libby used to have to watch out for him as he came swaggering down to the glovers' cottages on Corve Street every Saturday, and how he would stand over their mother, wetting his pencil in his mouth and smirking as he calculated the mean wages he owed them. She began to gather up the tea-cups and load the tray again. No, not sewn by a fairy, she thought bitterly as she backed towards the door, just a very small child as you ought to know, Mr Evans.

She shut the door quickly behind her so that she did

not have to listen to Mr Evans' slippery compliments or watch his swaying fat behind for another moment. If they only knew what that man was really like, she thought.

Downstairs, the kitchen was still hectic. Mrs Stringer grabbed her by the ear as soon as she came in.

"There you are, you lazy good-for-nothing. Don't you know there's work to be done?" She stopped suddenly, snapping her mouth shut like a trap. "Saucepans," she declared all of a sudden and when Annie frowned at her, she pulled her head around to face a mountain of blackened pots and pans by the stone sink. "Look smart about it, girl, and don't stop until they're all washed and hung up in their place."

It was a good hour before Annie had scrubbed and dried them and hung them up on their hooks above the range. Long before that, poor Sam the chimney-boy had got fed up waiting for his promised food to arrive and had wandered off to the Angel Inn to see if Israel Bessell was drunk enough to throw him a few pence.

Chapter 2

The smell of ammonia at the bottom of Corve Street was enough to skin the inside of your nose. It came from the tanners' yards which backed on to the river. Here the men dressed, cured, dried and cut up the leather hides for the glovers, soaking them first in great vats full of urine. Only the stink in the shambles, the part of town where the abattoir was, smelled worse. The glovers' cottages were in front of the tanners' yards. It was easy to tell which of the cottages in the row were the glovers' houses because there was a tier of overlapping wooden slats under the eaves of their roofs. Up there, in those top rooms, the leather skins were hung to dry on makeshift lines strung out above the heads of the women and children who hand-sewed and embroidered the gloves. The open slats made the room cold and draughty. The early morning mists which lay over the river at the back of the houses whistled under them, seeped into the walls, settled on the steaming leathers, and left a damp film on every surface. Libby Spears, Annie's little sister, and her mother, Kezia, worked, ate and slept in one of these upper rooms.

Libby was not yet five-years-old but she was already one of the best stitchers in the town, a town where nearly five hundred children under the age of ten worked for the wealthy glove merchants like Mr Evans, turning out beautiful hand-stitched and embroidered gloves that would be worn on some of the richest hands in the land.

On the table in front of her stood the donkeys, the wooden stands which held the work she still had to do before she could go to bed: three ladies' gloves. That meant fifteen fingers to sew, up and down and around, from the fifth little finger to the slender thumb, doing twelve tiny stitches to the inch, each one precisely the size of the one before it. Her fingers ached as she pushed her little needle through the fine cream kid leather, taking care not to puncture it or, worst of all, stain it with blood for she often pricked herself. Beside her on the bench, her mother embroidered the wrists of the gloves with fine gold thread, holding the material close up to her eyes, for working in bad light had made her sight poor and it was getting poorer all the time. The flame of the candles trembled in the draught.

Snip, snip, snip went her mother's scissors. Libby's eyelids drooped. She could hear outside the night owls calling to one another as they swooped down from the castle battlements to hunt along the banks of the river. She was hungry and the little ball of leather that she had been pushing around in her mouth had long since given out all its flavour. Down in the street, a cart trundled past, a horse whinnied and a dog barked far away. Her head jerked forwards. The glove she had been stitching fell to the floor beside her. She looked sideways at her mother to see if she had noticed. She sighed loudly.

Mrs Spears raised her head from her work and stroked Libby's cheek. "One more hour or two, Libby, and it will all be done. I promise."

"I'm tired."

"I know, pet. But the work must be done. It's collection day tomorrow and Mr Evans will be here looking for his rent."

"Why?"

Mrs Spears didn't answer. She pushed Libby's hair back from her forehead and placed the fallen glove back in her hand. Then, turning away from her daughter, she snipped the end of her thread, pinned the finished glove to the other half of the pair and laid them on the pile on the table in front of her.

"Come on, Libby, sit on the floor for a while and lean your back against the table leg. That way, you won't feel so sleepy."

"It's not my back. It's my fingers that ache. My feet feel fizzy. My eyes are sore."

"Poor Libby. Soon we can stop."

Libby's eyes filled with tears. She climbed down off her chair and sat rocking on her heels on the floor.

Downstairs there was a loud banging at the front door, four sharp knocks that showed the visitor meant to come in even though it was so late. Libby and her mother looked at each other in alarm.

"Mr Evans?" thought Kezia, wondering if she dared ignore his knocking. Would he be so bold as to call on her at this time of night? She wished her son William was there. Then came a shout from a familiar voice.

"It's Annie," cried Libby. "Annie has come home."

She jumped up, tossing the hated glove aside, and rushed down the stairs with her mother following close behind.

"They've let me come home for the night. I don't have to be back at Dinham until six in the morning," said Annie as soon as her mother and her sister had stopped kissing and hugging her and let her speak. "And I have something for you, three slices of sultana cake."

"Cake?" squealed Libby, who had eaten nothing that day but some oatmeal at mid-day.

"Then I shall make tea," said her mother, "and you can tell us all the news from Dinham House. It is so good to see you, my pet, after so many weeks. I have been so anxious for you, alone among all those strange people."

"Are there really princes and princesses where you work?" asked Libby, when they were back in the upstairs room.

"Oh yes, ever so many of them. First there are two daughters of Prince Lucien by his first wife who died. They are called Charlotte and Christine-Egypta. Then there are two younger girls, Letitia and Jeanne and two little boys, Charles and Paul-Marie. I often have to bathe the littlest one and put him to bed. And there are lots of other people too, a nephew and a French priest who has come to England with them, and they are all so noisy!

They all talk so loudly in their own language and sometimes they say things when I am in the room and they laugh and I go red. And, you know," she said, lowering her voice to a whisper, "the girls all wear beautiful silk dresses and their middles are never where their middles ought to be for they're cut high up on their chests or else low down on their hips with pretty sashes."

Annie rattled on, all her news tumbling out in a rush for she had hardly heard the sound of her own voice in the three weeks since she had started work. While her mother made the tea, she told them about bossy Mrs Stringer and Arthur, the friendly footman.

"And what do you do there?" asked Libby, picking out the currants from her slice of cake and popping them one by one into her mouth.

"Well," said Annie, thoughtfully. "First I clean the boots every morning – sometimes there are twenty pairs! Then I bring hot water up to the bedrooms and empty the chamber pots."

"Yuck," said Libby, grinning. "I wouldn't do that."

"You would if Mrs Stringer told you to. It's 'do this, do that, stop dawdling,' all day long. 'Annie Spears, take this tray, wash out those pots, polish those door handles, sweep out the kitchen floor and *get a move on*.'" She mimicked the fat housekeeper's whining voice.

"You're too thin, Annie," Kezia said when Annie finally stopped talking. "Are they not giving you enough to eat up there in that fancy house?"

Annie smiled. She was so pleased to be at home with her own family, listening to the familiar sound of the scissors snipping and the clack of her mother's thimble as she tapped it on the table, watching the snippets of leather and thread collecting on the floorboards as her sister worked. But she also saw Libby's peaked little white face, the dark circles under her eyes and her stifled yawns.

"I'm not thin, mother, just tired. I must have run up and down those kitchen stairs a hundred times today. Let's all go to bed. I could sleep and sleep."

Since they had told her she could go home for the night, she had been looking forward to lying under the quilt beside her little sister, listening to her quiet breathing, instead of Mrs Stringer's snoring or the weeping of the homesick French maids in the room next door.

"You go on to bed, Annie," her mother told her, "and have your rest, but Libby and myself must get on with our work."

"Oh, mother, have a heart and let Libby come to bed with me. You can see the poor mite is worn out."

"We cannot stop yet, Annie. All these gloves must be finished by morning for Evans will be here first thing to collect them. As it is, we have done only enough to cover the rent. We shall end up in the workhouse if we do not deliver all of these for I have nothing left to sell, neither furniture nor clothes. Nothing at all." She rubbed the empty space where her wedding ring should have been. Annie watched her mother's face, knowing she was thinking of her father, but said nothing.

"What time will William be back?" she asked after a while. "Surely he should be home by now?"

"Poor William won't be back until Saturday next at the earliest," said her mother.

"Oh," said Annie, "that means I won't see him for weeks."

"It's on account of all the orders for new hats that Mr Smart has got recently. William has to sleep over in the workshop in Quality Square until they have them all made up."

"That will be because of the ball," said Annie, pleased to pass on a bit of gossip. "Arthur told me there's going to be a ball at the Assembly Rooms next week with the Bonapartes invited: all Ludlow Society will be there."

"Well, thank God for Lucien Bonaparte, I say, for new hats for rich folk mean extra work for William and more money in our pockets. You mark my words, Annie and Libby too, we will hold our heads up high in this town again. We will never go cap in hand to the churchwarden asking for help like paupers. We may have to work till we drop, Annie, but we shall never set foot in that workhouse. Just three more years and the worst will be over."

Annie looked at her mother's tight angry face. "Have you heard any news of father?" she asked.

Her mother shook her head. "May God have mercy on him and keep him safe."

"Has there been no ship in at all with the mail?"

"Not a one. It's because of the war with France, they say. No ship has sailed for the Colony for months and the fleet that went to Australia last summer and that ought by rights to have got back by now was requisitioned at the Canary Islands on its way home and sent directly into battle. I daresay there's a letter on it that will reach us when the ship returns to Portsmouth. They say that the poor wretched convicts that are waiting to be transported are being press-ganged in to the Army to fight instead. Until they start sending ships to Australia again, we can expect no news."

"But it's been four years since he was sent away. Surely he could have got word out to us in all that time. Why does he not write?"

"Shush, Annie. If there was some way he could send a letter, believe me, he would. We don't know what it's like there in Botany Bay. Your father is a convict," Annie's mother's face darkened, "at least that is what they say he is, though God knows there was never a more honourable man in all of England. It may not be possible for him to get a letter sent out on the ships bound for London."

"Perhaps father is dead, mother," said Libby, who had been listening all the while without saying a word. She had been a baby when her father went away so she did not remember him at all. "Perhaps he got sick and died like Mr Evans always tells you. If you marry Mr Evans we should not have to sew gloves."

"What? Are you going to marry Mr Evans?" Annie looked at her mother in disbelief.

"Your father is not dead," said Kezia fiercely. "One day we will all be together again. His time will be up in three years and he will have his liberty."

"It's not fair," said Annie, "it's all Master Evans' fault."

Her mother measured out a length of linen, wet the end in her mouth and threaded her needle. She did not want any more of this talk. "If it hadn't been for Mr Evans, your father might have been hanged, Annie. And William would not have been able to go to the Grammar School. Remember that and try to think well of him for, without him, we would all have been in the workhouse."

Annie snorted. Four years earlier, her father, John Spears, a tanner, had been sentenced to hanging at the Shrewsbury Assizes for passing a forged banknote. It was only on account of a letter that Leonard Evans, the glove merchant, wrote to the judge asking for leniency, that his sentence was reduced. Instead of being hanged, he had been transported to the penal colony of New South Wales for seven years. The judge had not asked John Spears where he had got the banknote or he might have learned that Evans had given it to him in his wages.

In the four years that they had been alone in England, they had had only two letters, both almost in tatters now from having been read and re-read so often. They had been sent from the convict ship *Julius Caesar* before he left, telling his wife and children that he was to be sent into exile at the other end of the world.

"My heart is broken," he wrote, "at the thought of having to part from all of you whom I love so dearly. To be cut off and sent into exile without having done any wrong to anyone is very hard on me. Forgive me the shame I have brought upon you and believe in my innocence always. May God protect you my dear wife and children and be merciful to me."

When that letter came, Kezia Spears had written to everyone she could think of, from the Shrewsbury judge to the Prime Minister himself, asking to be allowed to travel out to Australia to join her husband. "Spare me the dishonour of throwing myself and my children at the mercy of the parish," she wrote, "for I have no means to gain a living but by what I can earn by my needle and the work is very poorly paid. In Sydney, my skills in dressmaking and glove-making may be of value to the colony."

Although a few families were sometimes allowed to travel out on the convict ships and start a new life in Australia, Kezia Spears' request was turned down. Before Annie's eighth birthday came around, she and her mother were working round the clock as glove-makers for Mr Evans. Libby, then only two, would not have to begin work for another couple of years.

In those early years, her brother William went to the school near the Mill Street Gate, with Mr Evans paying the fees, but what the glove merchant gave with one hand he took back with the other. The rent for the house in Corve Street was soon nearly as much as Kezia and Annie could earn with their sewing. They gave up the lower floor and moved into the one room upstairs. One Friday William threw down his slate and told his mother he had left school. At first he took a job as a servant for Abraham Smart and his wife in Quality Square, but within months they had made him their apprentice hat-maker.

"Give me a glove to hem," said Annie, at last, to her

mother, "and let me help you for I will not be able to sleep if you are still at work and the candles burning."

"It's not fair, Annie, my love," said Kezia. "You have your own work to do and an early start again in the morning."

"I'll be all right. Pass me a glove, Libby," said Annie, "and I'll give you a penny from my wages at Easter-time if you can finish yours faster than me."

No one spoke after that, but drew closer to sit in the pool of light cast by the tallow candle. They stitched and stitched until their fingers ached and their eyes were closing with weariness. It was long after the night watchman had gone past banging his staff against the cobbles and calling out "it's past one o'clock and a starlight morning" when they were finally able to lie down and sleep. Annie curled her body around the smaller body of her sister, but even when Libby finally fell asleep, Annie could sense that her fingers kept moving mechanically for several minutes as if she was still sewing the tiny leather fingers even though there was nothing in her hands at all. Annie drew her closer and held her hands in hers to stop them moving. After a while the nervous twitching stopped and Libby's breathing became deeper and peaceful at last.

In the other little bed tucked in between the window and the table, however, her mother still fretted. Annie could hear her coughing and tossing this way and that, pulling the blanket around her and bunching up the bundle of clothes she was using as a pillow as if she could not make herself comfortable enough to sleep. Now and then huge shadows crept around the walls as the night watchman walked by the house, waving his lantern in front of him to light his way.

Mother would surely never marry Mr Evans, thought Annie, pulling Libby closer to her. Please, she prayed, let there be a letter from father soon so that she will know he has not died.

In her dreams, she imagined she was on a convict ship bound for Australia. In the dark shadows below deck lay men and women chained together, their ankles in shackles so they could not walk. Faces loomed up in front of her, faces of men flogged to within an inch of their lives, of women riddled with fevers, of starving children begging for food. She was running from one to the other, handing out plates of cake, her body aching with exhaustion. "Spears," the familiar voice of Mrs Stringer was shouting, "Set that fire. Clean those boots. Fill that scuttle." The beautiful French princess, Christine-Egypta, was looking down on her from the crow's nest. "I know you are the daughter of a transport," she called to her.

"Papa," Annie shouted but when she woke, it was her mother who was holding her, rocking her back to sleep.

Chapter 3

"That odious little brat only went to the bend in the flue and settled down for a nap when I had him in to sweep my chimney the other day," remarked Leonard Evans, looking out the shop window as Sam Price, clutching a bundle of rags and brushes, trailed past behind Master Bessell. "Some of these children would sleep all day if they could and still whinge for their supper. I can tell you, I sent him off with a flea in his ear."

Abraham Smart placed Mr Evans' new top hat in its leather carrying-box and passed it across the counter.

"A flea in his ear, eh?" he said, peering over his half-moon glasses at his customer. Mr Smart was one of those people who neither agreed nor disagreed with anything people said to him but kept everybody quite happy by repeating the ends of their sentences. It seemed to do the trick. It also meant he didn't really have to pay attention to most of the conversation but could quietly get on with fastening the buckle on a hat or giving the crown a final brushing.

"That hat is a beauty, I grant you that, Mr Smart," said Mr Evans, picking up the leather box. "As fine a hat as ever I've seen."

"There is nothing like a fine tall hat to give a man stature," agreed Mr Smart, proudly, "and that specimen is all of nine inches from brim to crown. You will stand above the crowd, Mr Evans, the very pillar of society."

"The hat is a credit to your craft, to be sure. And now I shall bid you good-day. Shall we be seeing you tonight at the Assembly Rooms?"

"At the Assembly Rooms? Yes, indeed, sir. Mrs Smart would give me no peace if she could not be there and see prince Bonaparte in person, or rather, see all the French ladies in the latest finery from Europe."

"Until this evening, then." Mr Evans gathered up his hat box and umbrella and departed.

No sooner had he closed the door than William Spears came out into the front shop from the workshop behind.

"Has he gone then, Master Smart? I daren't be in the same room as that man for fear I might let myself fly at him."

Mr Smart the hatter squinted at William over the top of his spectacles. He was a tall thin man, about sixty years old, and very stooped like someone who had spent his life trying to make believe he was not as tall as he truly was. He was mostly bald, though he still had tufts of hair over his ears and wild sprouting eyebrows that were stained reddish-brown from the solution of mercury he used to brush the beaver fur of his hats. Those same fumes of mercury, breathed in year after year, had also affected his brain, people said, so that he was gradually losing his wits, becoming quite mad as hatters were inclined to do.

"My dear Wills," he said, "you will never make any money if you think like that. When a gentleman is in trade, he will do business with old Nick himself."

"Well, I would not care to do business with him. It was he who has ruined my family," said William, vehemently.

"Ruined your family?" said the hatter, "If that is so, and I'm not disagreeing with you, it's up to you to 'unruin' them. And hats is the way to do it. Does Sam Price wear a topper?"

William nodded. He had heard this argument a dozen times a day for the best part of two years.

"And would Lord Powis be seen with a bare head?"

William shook his head.

"There you have the secret of a good business. Make or sell something that everybody needs, from the highest lord in the land to the lowest chimney sweep's skivvy." Mr Smart tapped the side of his head. "They may say I am mad, William Spears, but my head is screwed on tighter than most. Now fetch the boxes and we'll pack up the hats for Dinham House. But first let us drink a toast to good King George."

He took a bottle of wine and two blue glasses from under the counter.

"God save His Majesty, William," he said, carefully pouring out a full glass for himself and a rather less full one for William, "a mad king, so they say, but a blessing to all hatmakers."

Mr Smart had taken to drinking a toast to King George each afternoon as, slowly but surely, the hat business he had set up at the turn of the century had started to grow. In those early days most men still wore wigs. Then the government had brought in a tax on wig powder. Since most people, men and women, both rich and poor, hate to pay a tax if there is any way around it, wigs went rapidly out of fashion and the hat came in instead. Mr Smart's business took off. Now, apart from some crusty old clergymen and the lawyers down at the courthouse who hung on to their powdery white wigs, everyone wore a hat.

Mr Smart was an acknowledged master of the craft. He made toppers, tapering or straight-sided, chimney-pot or stove-pipe, black beaver or silk plush, broad-brimmed or narrow-brimmed, fawn or purple, brown or black. He had recently designed a prototype hat that collapsed in on itself, ideal for a man to stick under his seat at the opera. He had thought about making papier mâché hats for those who could not afford fur or silk – but hadn't yet solved the problem about going out in the rain. The man was unquestionably the king of the hatters in Ludlow and far beyond. Earlier that year he had sent a selection of his hats to the royal court in London – William was sure they had never been ordered, let alone paid for. In any case, Mr Smart had *Hat-Maker to the King* written in gold lettering on his hat-boxes. His latest plan was to fit out Lucien Bonaparte and his entourage in Smart hats and add *Hat-Maker to European Royalty*. It was difficult to know if it would be good or bad for business to boast of the Bonaparte connection.

Business was the thing and Mr Smart, for all his dottiness, was good at it. "There's a great future to be had for hatters, William," he said, topping up his glass with another couple of inches of wine. He had to clutch the bottle with both hands for the mercury poisoning was giving him the shakes. "You stick to this trade with me and you and your sisters will never know the meaning of hunger again."

William drained his glass in one and gathered up the order of hats for Dinham House. "Your good health, Mr Smart."

"And yours, Wills." He placed a shilling on the counter and pushed it towards William. "Take that and buy something extra for your supper. And wrap up warm. There's a keen wind coming in from the east today. I wouldn't be surprised if you see people skating down on the river. It's the coldest January I can remember for many a long year."

Outside, William piled up the hat-boxes on the hand-cart he used to make his deliveries in the town. The cold air made him gasp when he came out of the shop into the courtyard. He had been so busy for the previous few days that he had not been outside at all and was astonished to discover that the world had turned white. It hadn't been snowing – it was too cold for that. Every building in Quality Square, from stable to workshop to warehouse, was rimmed with white frost. Short icicles hung from under the eaves of the stables and the edges of window-sills were sprinkled with brittle frosting. The ground underfoot was solid, for the usual mud that had been churned up by horses' hooves and the rains at the beginning of the year had frozen into uneven ruts and ridges that made pushing the handcart hard-going.

As he came out under the archway into Castle Square, William stopped to look around him. The London stagecoach had just drawn up in front of the White Horse Inn and a bailiff was taking delivery of the mail bag. The horses, sweating hard after the final descent into the town, were snorting great plumes of hot breath that instantly turned to icy droplets. Leonard Evans, with his new hat box under his arm, was swaying across the square in the direction of the mail coach. William could see the bailiff holding something out to him.

Otherwise, the scene seemed unnaturally still as if the cold snap had slowed everyone down. The market traders, shifting their weight from one foot to the other to keep their blood circulating, looked pinched and miserable under their heavy shapeless coats. Even the man at the fish bench at the rear of the Market Hall, crying out that he had oysters from the Welsh coast, three pence the dozen, sounded bored by his own voice. It was getting dark, almost time to shut up for the night.

William trundled his cart over the cobbles of the square and round by the castle walls to Dinham House where Lucien Bonaparte had taken up residence. The house was a large, handsome red-brick one, one of the finest in all of Ludlow, built right up against the outer walls of the ancient castle. He rang the bell at the side entrance and began to unload the hats from the cart. The carillon clock in the tower of the parish church began to ring out as he was waiting for the door to open. It was four o' clock in the afternoon. The house with the curtains drawn seemed deserted. He rang again. He stamped his feet and whistled. It was so quiet, even the river which usually tumbled noisily over the weir a few hundred yards away was eerily silent. William guessed that Mr Smart was right and that it must be frozen over.

Behind him, there was a clatter of loose stones and the squawk of a jackdaw as it rose up from the castle walls. A rat, thought William, picking up a rock to throw at it, if it appeared. There was more scrabbling and scratching. He thought he heard someone moaning and called out, "who's there?" Just then, a pool of yellow candlelight appeared behind the window next to the door and the butler's face peered out at him. In a trice, he handed over his order, took the receipt, and was just about to turn down the hill to see the frozen river when he saw the figure of his sister Annie disappearing down the basement steps.

"Hey, Annie," he shouted, catching up with her in the nick of time before she vanished behind the heavy wooden doors. Annie turned around, her face lit up with pleasure at seeing her brother for they had not seen each other since she had started her new job as parlour-maid in Dinham.

"Come down to the river with me, Annie. If it's frozen

hard enough, I'll give you a ride out on the ice on my handcart."

Annie's face fell with disappointment. "Oh, William, I wish I could but I daren't leave or Mrs Stringer will box my ears. Everyone in the house is going to the ball tonight. The French maids are busy dressing the ladies and I have to help with the little ones' supper and get them to bed."

William looked at his little sister. She looked gaunt and worn out. "Are you all right, Annie? Are they good to you in there? I haven't seen you since you started."

"I'm all right, William, but it is hard being away from home. They let me spend one night there last week but . . ." her voice trailed off.

William raised an eyebrow.

"But what?" he asked.

"Mother is so unhappy because papa doesn't write and Libby looks ill."

"What do you mean, ill?"

"She's too small for the work and the hours she has to do. Mother and Libby sew and sew and still earn scarcely enough to pay the rent, let alone have anything left over for food. What's worse is I think Evans wants to marry Mother."

"Evans marry mother? She wouldn't! She couldn't! Father is still alive." William gripped Annie's elbow.

"But say he is dead? It's well known that half the convicts die on the ships."

"You must not believe that, Annie. A letter will come soon, you'll see, and Mr Smart will give me my dues at

36

the end of the month so we shall not be so badly off. I'll talk to mother – if she can hold out just a little longer, everything will be all right. You know how father loved us all. We'll hear from him soon, I am sure of it."

Behind them, in the dark shadows beneath the castle wall, there was more scrabbling and another shower of small stones fell to the ground.

"What *is* that?" said William, sharply.

"Nothing, just old stones falling down from the tower."

"No," said William. "Listen."

For a moment, they could hear nothing but the distant clip-clop of a horse's hooves as a carriage crossed the bridge. Then, quite clearly, they heard a sneeze, and then another.

William frowned at Annie and put his finger to his lips. He tiptoed towards the wall: deep in the shadows sat Sam Price, clutching a clump of grass and rubbing his knees.

"What are you doing here, Sam Price?" demanded William.

"Trying to climb up," said Sam.

"Into the castle? But there's nothing in there. It's all in ruins," said William.

"I know," answered Sam, "but I've got to hide somewhere. I've run away."

"You clot," said William. "Where do you think you can hide in a town this size?"

"I'm not going to stay in Ludlow. I'm running away to sea. I'm not going to work another day for Bessell. See what he gave me?" He pointed at a cut under his eye. "And all because I spilt a bag of soot on Mistress Allen's best rug."

William whistled. He looked from Sam's small sooty face to his sister's.

"Well, Annie," he said, solemnly, "is there anywhere in all of Dinham where we can stow this young man away until his ship comes in?"

"Yes," said Annie, thinking quickly. "Come on. I'll show you."

Chapter 4

Lucien Bonaparte was a light eater but a fussy one. He had always tended to have indigestion but the condition had got steadily worse. Ever since he had fallen out with his brother, the emperor Napoleon, and put himself in self-imposed exile, he had felt unsafe. For years war had been spreading all over the Mediterranean and beyond as his brother's ambitions grew. Lucien had had to become suspicious, until he was hardly able to tell the difference between friend or foe. It had done his stomach no good.

Eight months earlier, he had boarded a ship at Civitavecchia in Northern Italy to sail with his family to the newly independent United States of America. But the British Navy had run him down, afraid that he would plot against them once he arrived in America. For months he and all his household had been held as prisoners of war in Malta. Then, for reasons he could not understand, they had brought him to England. He was a free man, yet not a free man. He could write his poetry, attend a ball or take supper with the leading families of Ludlow – but he could not leave. He could not send or receive mail without allowing a lieutenant-colonel of the British Army to read it. He looked out his bedroom window at the frozen limbs of the trees on Whitcliffe Common opposite, at the clammy ribbon of fog which lay down in the hollows of the river valley and shuddered, remembering the golden light of Rome. His stomach rumbled. He rang the bell for his personal cook to bring him a light supper before going out to the ball. He did not yet trust the English to feed him.

The kitchens of Dinham House at five o'clock were far from quiet. All hands were on deck for there was dinner to be made for the children and the servants themselves, a late supper to be got ready and served at midnight after the ball was over, and tea and small cakes to be taken upstairs at once to the music room for all the young ladies and the tutor and the chaplain and Madame Alexandrine herself. A large ham was rattling in an iron pot on the stove and a plucked goose lay on a table waiting to be stuffed. The cook was standing over a bowl with flour up to her elbows, mixing pastry for the hot mince pies. Every so often, she glanced with a look that could kill at the Frenchman's personal cook. He had taken two of the brown speckled eggs she had been keeping back for her own supper, not to mention a bottle of the best brandy from the cellar, and was making up some strange concoction to calm Prince Lucien's stomach. Maids, butlers and footmen flew in and out with trays.

In the midst of all this commotion, Annie arrived back unnoticed. She had sent Sam to hide overnight in an outhouse next to the stables and William had agreed to come back in the morning to take him up to the abandoned shepherd's hut above Whitcliffe. After that, he would have to take his own chances. Ludlow was a long way from the sea. In the meantime, Annie had promised to find him something to eat for he had had nothing all day.

There was a tray sitting on a side-table, already laid out with a china plate, a set of silver cutlery and a glass of wine. Though Annie didn't know it, it was the tray the French cook had been getting ready for Lucien. She picked it up and walked as confidently as she could to the pantry. She took a chicken drumstick, a large spoonful of potted rabbit, a small wheaten loaf and a wedge of cheese. Then, hardly daring to breathe in case someone asked her what she was doing and where she was going, she nipped out through the scullery, past the well-room and out to the shed next to the castle wall where Sam Price was hiding.

Sam heard the footsteps coming near and pressed himself against the wall. It was pitch-dark but he was used to the dark. He didn't like it, but he wasn't afraid of it any more as he had been when he had first been forced up the chimneys. At least, here in the shed, he could move around or stretch out his legs when he wanted, not like up some chimneys where he could hardly wriggle through the opening and he was in constant terror that his shoulders would jam in some narrow flue. His greatest fear was that one day he would be stuck forever, unable to move either up or down. The door creaked open.

"Sam?" whispered Annie.

"Here," answered Sam, pushing the door back. With his sooty face and clothes, he was almost invisible but for the whites of his eyes and his teeth.

"I've brought you supper, but you must stay here and eat it in the dark for I didn't dare take a candle. I'll come back later for the tray."

"And can you bring a blanket? It's bitter cold in here."

"You don't ask for much, do you?" said Annie, annoyed. "Do you know what trouble I would be in if I was caught pinching that food for you? Just be grateful I haven't gone to tell Master Bessell where you are."

"Oh, Annie, you'd never tell on me, would you? I was only joking about the blanket. Have a sip of my wine." He grinned lopsidedly, for he had recently lost another two baby teeth, and held out the glass to her.

"Do you think he's found out you have gone and is out looking for you?" asked Annie, mollified.

"Who knows? As likely as not, he'll be drinking all evening in the Mug House and won't know I've gone until he wants me to take his boots off at bedtime. I have to get out of Ludlow, Annie, for he'll kill me if he catches me."

"And how are you going to do that? Everyone knows you to see. And Bessell will put up a reward for you."

"Nah, he's too mean for that," Sam said thoughtfully,

picking up the chicken drumstick and licking it, "but he might come after me."

"Where will you go? Have you no family?"

"I expect there's some round Diddlebury that know me but none that would take me in. My father gave me away to Master Bessell, or sold me most probably, a couple of years back. I daren't go back there."

"He sold you?"

Sam nodded. "One night in the Elephant & Castle. First thing I knew about it was being shaken out of bed and told to get my clothes on."

"But didn't your mother stop them?"

"I haven't got a mother," said Sam, matter-of-factly. "She died the same day I was born. I'm going to go to Bristol, Annie, to get a job on a ship as a cabin boy." His eyes were shining in the darkness. "Have you ever seen the sea, Annie? I saw a painting of it once in a house I was working in. It's blue, blue as the sky, and it goes on for ever and ever."

"No, I never saw the sea, nor am I sure I'd want to if it goes on for ever and ever. They sent my father over the sea and nobody has ever heard from him since."

Outside, carriage wheels rolled over the cobbles. The horses snorted. Their hooves clattered in the rear courtyard as the coachmen shunted them into their harnesses.

"Listen, Sam, do you hear that? They're bringing up the carriages to take everyone to the ball. I have to go back in. Mrs Stringer will be looking for me." She put her finger up to her lips. "You must be quiet as a mouse,

Sam Price, or someone will hear you and then we'll both be in trouble. I'll be back as soon as I can. There's probably some stuff in here you can wrap yourself up in if you get cold. Just remember, not a sound."

Chapter 5

Libby was home alone.

A cattleman had called earlier to say there was a letter for Mrs Kezia Spears just come in on the mail coach from London.

"I just happened to be in the square when the coach came in," the man explained. "I heard the bailiff shout across to Master Evans, 'You're Kezia Spears' landlord, aren't you?' he said. 'Well, there's a letter here for her you might want to give her.' I saw William was just on the other side of the square. He was coming out from Quality Square with his handcart all piled up with hat boxes and I thought Evans might have called him over but he just put the letter in his pocket without even looking at it and marched off. I reckoned you might want to go and fetch it right away," he went on, rather embarrassed. "I expect it'll be from John, won't it?"

Libby's mother could not believe her ears. She went all to pieces. There was only one person in the whole wide world who would send her a letter for she knew no one outside of Ludlow. It had to be from John, alive and thinking of her still after the long years of silence.

"This is the best news I have heard for many a year! A thousand times thank you!" Kezia said, "but where is the letter now? Where can I go to fetch it?"

"Evans is going to the ball, isn't he? I daresay you'd find him if you go to Castle Square. I'd walk up there with you myself but I'm off to Hereford market in the morning and still have the cart to load up."

"Libby," Kezia had said to her daughter when the man had gone, "will you wait here for me and be a good girl? It's too cold to take you out on a night like this and I shall get up to the square and back faster if I go alone."

Libby's bottom lip had turned inside out.

"No, Libby," said Kezia, warningly. "You mustn't act like a baby. You've nothing warm enough to wear out on a bitter night like this. You stay here and finish stitching that glove. I'll be back before the candle's half way burnt down."

She undid her apron and folded it on the table. As Libby looked on with wide frightened eyes, her mother pulled on her coat and wrapped another shawl around her head and shoulders. "I will only be gone for a few minutes, Libby," she pleaded. "Then, when I get back, we'll read the letter from your father and have our supper."

"Does this mean you won't have to marry Mr Evans?" Libby asked.

Kezia kissed her tiny daughter on the top of the head. "Don't worry, my pet, I will not marry Mr Evans." She lit a fresh candle and placed it in the centre of the table.

"Ten minutes, my love, and I'll be back."

Libby heard the heavy iron key turn in the keyhole and her mother's light steps going down the stairs to the street. At first she sewed a little more of the glove she was working on but with no one to watch over her, she soon got bored and threw it aside.

I hate gloves, she thought, with feeling. When I am big, I shall never wear them.

The room was so cold even the insides of the windows had frosted over. She clambered up on to a window-sill, and cleared a small round peephole in one of the panes so that she could keep a watch for her mother's return. The street was empty. The wooden slats beneath the eaves rattled in the cold east wind. The leather skins hanging above her head trembled in the breeze. The tallow candle in its saucer tilted and fell over. With her back to the table, Libby did not notice the flame of the candle licking around the discarded glove, catching the apron strings, running along the table cloth, spreading down the leg of the table. By the time she smelled the smoke, it was too late, the wooden floor was ablaze. There was no way out.

The Ball in honour of Ludlow's distinguished visitors was to be held in the Assembly Rooms, the long hall that occupied the upper storey of the tumble-down

Market Hall in the Castle Square. It was not that the hall itself was tumble-down. A great deal of public money had been lavished upon it. New glass chandeliers had recently been installed and its springy dancing floor would not have been out of place in a more important city like Bath or even London. People in Ludlow liked to think that nobody could find fault with their orchestra, a band of men who could rise to any occasion. And if they didn't always know the tune or the beat to the bar, you had to admit that they were always willing to please.

Nevertheless, stangers to Ludlow were never very enthusiastic at the sight of the Assembly Rooms. The lower part of the building was occupied during the day by the market traders so it smelled of fish and cabbages and barnyard manure. Most of the ball-goers that night arrived up the stairs with fans fluttering and handkerchiefs clamped to their wrinkled noses.

Everybody who was anybody was there: the aldermen and councillors, with their wives, all the best families of the town and neighbourhood, the Sneades and Charltons, the judges, the lawyers, the merchants. There was even a lord or two and a bishop. The square was chock-a-block with carriages arriving and departing, their owners shouting out last minute instructions about when the drivers should return. The poor were out in force too, milling around the doors of the White Horse Inn and the carriage set-down points, hoping to earn a tip or two by holding the reins of the horses, or simply gawking at the finery of the ladies.

Kezia Spears could not get through the crowds. Women elbowed her out of the way as she tried to steer a path towards the inn, thinking she was pushing in front of them to get a better view of the French princesses' ball gowns. There was an ugly mood in the air. A lot of soldiers were in the town, among them war veterans at a loss to know why, in the middle of the war with France, the brother of the tyrant Napoleon was being honoured in Ludlow. Some of these men had served under Admiral Nelson at the great Battle of Trafalgar six years earlier; some had lost limbs, others had lost their hearing from the booming of the cannons and were still stone deaf. They did not know Lucien and his family were under parole, a form of house arrest – they just heard the hated name Napoleon and wondered if the sacrifices they had made were all in vain.

When the first of the carriages from Dinham House drew up and Lucien Bonaparte and his wife Alexandrine stepped down, a huge jeer went up from the crowd of men standing at the front door of the White Horse.

"Long live the Royal Navy."

"Remember Trafalgar."

"Down with Napoleon Bonaparte."

"Hurray to that. And down with France."

A party of militiamen rushed forward into the crowd, bayonets drawn, seized the hecklers and hustled them away. Lucien Bonaparte coldly ignored the disturbance. He steered his wife and daughters past a noxious heap of rotting cabbage stalks and led them up the staircase to the Long Hall.

Kezia squeezed past the crowds into the tap-room of the White Horse. The bar was full of coachmen and ostlers who pressed up against her and made lewd remarks when she asked the innkeeper where she might find Mr Evans. The air was blue and thick with the smell of tobacco smoke and spilt ale. The breath of the customers was stale and sour and the atmosphere was still threatening as if more trouble might break out at any moment. The master glover was nowhere to be seen. Dejectedly, Kezia began to push her way back out on to the street.

In the few minutes that she had been inside the inn, the crowds of people had moved away from the square. The sightseers and gawpers were no longer hanging around the entrance to the Assembly Rooms but had drifted to the other end of the High Street. People were craning their necks, trying to see over the heads of those in front.

"The fire engine's been called out from the parish church," she heard someone say.

". . . a house down by the Corve . . ."

"It's one of the tanners' cottages," said a man in front of her.

In the far distance she could hear the clanging of the night watchman's bell and the shouts of "Fire! fire!"

"Let me past," she screamed, all interest in her letter forgotten. "I must get past."

People plucked at her shawl and sleeves to hold her back but she pushed against them and forced her way out of the crowd. She picked up her skirt and ran, sliding and slipping on the icy cobbles, straight through the dark lanes, round by the Bull Ring, on past the brightly-lit Feathers Hotel, and down the hill towards the terrace of black-and-white timbered cottages. As she got nearer, she could see the red glow in the sky, the tell-tale jets of sparks, could smell the acrid smell of burning wood. It was her house that was on fire.

The road was blocked by three fire-engines, their horses and crews. Two of the crews were standing idly by, enjoying the spectacle. They were from the fire insurance companies and would not help out once they had seen that there was no brass plaque on the wall to show that fire insurance had been taken out on the house. The other one belonged to the parish and would come out to assist at any fire, whether for a pauper or a rich man. Two of its crew were feeding out the canvas and leather hose while two others stood either side of the manual pump, trying in vain to pump up water from the river Corve which ran behind the house. The river had frozen solid. Kezia's neighbours were kneeling on the bank, frantically hammering at the ice with pick-axes to get to the water beneath. Several empty leather buckets lay uselessly on the bank.

Kezia stood outside her home, screaming Libby's name. The women from the cottages round about had come out on to the street. Several of them tried to hold her back from the flames, but she covered her head with her shawl and plunged headlong into the blazing house.

There was a slow steady splintering noise which grew louder and louder. A huge beam swung out from the house and fell into the road with a sickening thud. The house collapsed in upon itself.

Chapter 6

Annie and William stood shoulder to shoulder in the damp cemetery beside the graves of their mother and little sister. The queue of mourners had filed past, one long sorrowful face after another, shaking their hands and telling the children how sorry they were for their trouble. Afterwards they gathered in small whispering groups behind the monuments of long-dead Ludlovians, or outside the graveyard gates, cheerfully exchanging their versions of how the fire broke out. Somehow the story had spread that Kezia had gone to have a look at Alexandrine Bonaparte. The shoemaker declared that it was no more than her just deserts for leaving her daughter alone while she went to gawp at toffs in their finery. A laundress from Frog Lane knew for a fact that Libby had always been in the habit of playing with fire while Walter Lloyd, the sexton, said the family had all gone to the bad. Wasn't John Spears as rotten as last year's windfalls? If it was ever true that virtue was rewarded and ill deeds punished, then you need look no further than the Spears. They were a bad lot.

Luckily, Annie and William did not hear any of these lies. They were numb with grief, shrinking within themselves, wishing only that they were dead too. They could not understand why Libby had been locked in the house alone for they knew nothing of the letter that their mother had gone in vain to pick up and the only man who could tell them, other than Leonard Evans himself, was the cattleman who had called to Kezia – and he had already left for Hereford. They only knew that they were now utterly alone in the world, with no one but each other to care what would become of them.

"Are you coming then, Annie?" Mrs Stringer took hold of Annie's shoulder and began to lead her away. "Say good-bye to your brother, girl."

"Where are you taking her?" asked William, taking Annie's other arm. He was shocked that they were to be separated again so soon. He had hardly had a chance to speak alone with her since the Reverend Gwynn had come with the news the night before to the hat factory.

"Back to Dinham House, of course," Mrs Stringer replied. "What is there to do but carry on working till the parish decides what is to be done with you and your sister. It'll stop her brooding. Life must go on." Mrs Stringer did not mean this to sound unkind. She had herself lost four children and a husband in the cholera epidemic of 1803. She reckoned she would have lost the will to live herself if she had not kept herself busy.

"What do you mean *until the parish decides?* Decides what?" said William, indignantly.

"Well," Mrs Stringer began uncertainly, "I expect the guardians may want to put you in the workhouse."

"The workhouse?" exclaimed William and Annie together. "Why should they do that?"

"I'm not saying that is what they are going to do, William. Only that they might. On account of your being homeless orphans."

"We are not orphans," said William.

Mrs Stringer sniffed. "As good as orphans, for what use is your father to you in a penal colony at the far side of the world? Where is he now to rear you and bring you up like Christians?"

William and Annie stared at her with loathing.

"We have our work," said William. "We do not need the parish."

Mrs Stringer's eyes narrowed. "Only as long as Bonaparte stays in Ludlow and there is work for Annie at Dinham," she said, "and, as for yourself, William Spears, it is well known that Abraham Smart is not fit to look after anyone. Everyone knows he is mad."

"Our mother said we should never have to go to the workhouse," declared Annie, looking towards her brother for support.

"No, and nor shall we," agreed William. "We'd rather run away to London and take our chances there. And Abraham Smart is no madder than you are."

Mrs Stringer pursed her lips. But for the yellow beard,

she thought, young Spears had a look of his father about him, another criminal in the making.

"I expect Master Smart will be wondering where you've got to, young man," she said, sharply. "Annie, come along now and dry those eyes."

Annie tramped after Mrs Stringer, feeling as miserable as it is possible to be. In less than twenty-four hours she had lost everything, her mother, her little sister, her home and possibly even her brother for if they were to be put in the workhouse, he would be with the men and she with the women. All that lay ahead of her now was skivvying, her days spent from first light until long past sunset fetching and carrying, running up and downstairs answering to the calls of master, mistress and all the other servants who ranked above her for she was the very least, the lowest, meanest thing in the whole household.

"Come along there, Annie Spears." Mrs Stringer had stopped in the road ahead of her and was waving her arms frantically for her to catch up. "There's screaming coming from the grounds. What can it all mean?" The housekeeper broke into a clumsy run around the castle walls towards Dinham House. Annie picked up her skirt and raced past her for she had recognised the screams at once. They were coming from Sam Price.

The outhouse door between the house and the castle wall was swinging open. Annie ran towards it. The screams got louder. Inside the shed, one of the French manservants had taken hold of Sam by the back of his shirt and the seat of his trousers. He had him dangling at arm's length, trying to avoid the boy's thrashing legs.

"Put me down," shouted Sam. "Put me down."

The Frenchman was shouting too at the top of his voice, a babble of exotic words that neither Annie nor Mrs Stringer could understand. When he saw that he had an audience, he lowered Sam to the ground and dragged him into the courtyard.

"He bit me, the little animal."

"I never did," shouted Sam, kicking out again at the servant's legs and catching him right in the shin.

A window on the first floor of Dinham House was abruptly thrown open and Lucien Bonaparte's head and shoulders appeared above them. Even Sam, seeing his black expression, had sense enough to shut up.

"What is this commotion? How can a man write with all this noise? Be quiet at once."

The manservant, still holding Sam firmly by the back of his collar, launched into a lengthy explanation.

"This boy was trespassing," he declared. "I found him asleep under a pile of rags in the shed. When I discovered him, he attacked me. What do you want me to do with him?"

"He's the chimney sweep's boy, your excellency," said Mrs Stringer, bobbing awkwardly on her fat legs, "I daresay the ungrateful boy has run away."

Bonaparte looked from his own affronted servant to the stout red-faced Mrs Stringer.

"I just want peace and quiet, Madame. Is it too much to ask?" His tummy was particularly bad that morning. He burped an acid blast of air out the window.

Mrs Stringer opened her mouth to speak but Lucien put up a hand to stop her.

"Get rid of him."

Mrs Stringer dipped down in another lop-sided curtsey. "Begging your pardon, sir. I shall send a message to Master Bessell, the sweep, and tell him to come and take the boy away directly." She reached out and gave Sam a cuff around the ears to show Lucien she had the measure of the local ruffians. The window up above shut with a decisive bang.

"Don't send me back to Mr Bessell, please, ma'am," Sam implored. "I promise I'll clear off. I won't bother you again." He looked across at Annie with eyes filled with tears. "I was waiting for William to come," he said, "He told me he'd show me where the shepherd's hut is."

"He couldn't come. Sam, my mother and Libby are dead. There was a fire in my house last night," Annie said to him. "William and I have just come from the graveyard."

Sam struggled out of the Frenchman's grasp and launched himself at Annie but Mrs Stringer, warily watching the upstairs window, would not allow them to speak any longer. "Go on in to the kitchen," she said brusquely, poking Annie in the back. "Tell the cook I'm back and that I shall be wanting a cup of tea to revive me after all this trouble."

Annie gripped Sam's small dirty hand and hurried him towards the basement steps.

"Annie," he whispered, patting the crown of his top hat to steady it firmly over his ears, "the next time I run away, no one will ever catch me."

Chapter 7

The freezing weather gave way soon after that to heavy rain that burst the banks of both the Teme and Corve rivers at Ludlow and churned up the streets and squares into a quagmire of mud. Annie rarely left Dinham House, except early on Sunday mornings, when Mrs Stringer took her to the parish church of St Laurence. Each week she sat in one of the back pews, straining to catch a glimpse of William but, if he was there, she never saw him. She had had no news of Sam since the afternoon Mr Bessell the sweep had dragged him screaming from the kitchen at Dinham.

The Bonaparte household had settled down to a sort of routine, with its own rhythms. Lucien spent the best part of his day studying – he was writing an epic poem about Charlemagne – while the younger children worked with their French tutor on their reading and writing or had English conversation classes with a local scholar. Madame Bonaparte and the two eldest girls were much in demand by the ladies of the town and soon were in the habit of going to take tea in the grand houses of Broad Street. In the afternoons they played cards in the parlour or took dancing lessons. Lucien's eldest step-daughter was thought to be the most beautiful creature in Ludlow and it was not long before rumours started that she was to marry one of the Charltons, a young man of considerable landed property. So, for a time at least, all was well. If it was a sort of imprisonment, Lucien and Alexandrine agreed, it was not too uncomfortable. In the evenings they arranged little concerts in the music room for themselves and their visitors or went to the theatre at the bottom of Mill Street where an extraordinary American actress, the beautiful Miss Constance Brooks, was playing Hippolyta, Queen of the Amazons, to full houses. The minor disturbances outside the Assembly Rooms on the night of the ball were forgotten.

Paul-Marie, the baby, had picked up some English words.

"Annie," he said, looking up at the long staircase as Annie led him out to take him to bed, and holding his hands up above his head, "carry me". He could not yet say his r's properly.

"No," she said, "you're too heavy. Walk."

"Carry."

"No. Walk."

"Annie carry." He smiled doubtfully. Then his lower lip turned out. He opened his mouth but no sound came out. His face had turned quite red.

"Breathe," pleaded Annie, grabbing him under his arms and running up the stairs. When the wailing finally came, it was loud enough to bring Christine-Egypta running from her bedroom on the first floor.

"What is it? What has happened?"

"Nothing, miss, he is all right," Annie stammered. The din that Paul-Marie was making made it impossible to say any more. He was thrashing around, hitting out at her face with tight angry fists. It hurt more than you would have thought. Annie leant away from him and patted his back, desperate for him to calm down. "I didn't do anything," she said, embarrassed.

"Give him to me," said Christine-Egypta, taking him roughly from Annie. "Be quiet at once," she commanded him in French, and instantly, the baby stopped the racket.

"You see, he is just being *méchant*."

Annie looked puzzled.

"Naughty." The French girl smiled at her. "Come, I have something to show you."

She beckoned at Annie to follow her into her bedroom. Annie hesitated. "Come," Christine-Egypta repeated.

In the bedroom, Christine-Egypta undid the catch of a tiny jewellery box on her dressing-table and drew out a gold locket.

"Look," she said, opening the miniature heart and holding it out for Annie to see. The locket held a little picture. It was the face of a young woman, beautiful and delicate, as pretty as Christine-Egypta herself.

"Is it you?" asked Annie shyly.

"No, she is my mother. Catherine-Christine Boyer was her name. She died when I was very small."

"My mother is dead too," said Annie.

"I know," said Christine-Egypta. "I heard Arthur and Mrs Stringer talking about you. You must be very sad."

Annie nodded. She was afraid that she might cry. "My little sister was killed too," she said.

Downstairs there was a loud ringing of bells and a shout from Mrs Stringer.

"Annie Spears, where are you?"

"Go, Annie Spears," said Christine-Egypta, smiling, "I will take Paul-Marie to bed."

Annie dipped a little curtsey and went running from the room.

A few days later at the beginning of March, the peaceful atmosphere in Dinham House was shattered. News had reached England that the British fleet had suffered great losses in battle against the emperor Napoleon Bonaparte. There were mounting rumours that he was planning to invade England while its army and navy were occupied fighting alongside the Spanish. As these stories spread, the people of Ludlow looked at Dinham House and wondered just what Lucien Bonaparte was doing there. Until then, most people had paid little attention to Lucien and his family. He minded his business. They minded theirs. Even the wasters and ne'er-do-wells who hung around the doors of the inns had got used to seeing the exotic visitors on their daily walks around the castle walls and rarely turned up to jeer or gawp at them. But, from one day to the next, the mood in the town turned ugly.

It seemed to have started with a number of sheep farmers arguing in the square one market day. They were discontent, as farmers were always inclined to be. The ones who were looking to buy sheep thought the prices were too high and the quality of the beasts poor, while those who were selling declared they were being robbed and forced to undersell their ewes and lambs. Their rumblings spread to other passers-by. The price of wheat was shocking. King George was mad. The Prince Regent was a scoundrel. There were louder mutterings that this interminable war against the French was impoverishing the entire country. It dragged on and on from year to year with no sign of victory. Napoleon Bonaparte was a scourge upon the whole of Europe.

"And yet," said a voice, "That tyrant's brother, Lucien Bonaparte, is a guest in our kingdom."

"Not just in our kingdom," said another, "but in our town."

That afternoon the children's tutor came home outraged that he and his charges had been insulted by ruffians when they were strolling in the castle grounds. The abbé, Lucien's personal chaplain, was spat at as he walked down by the river. The same evening, after dark, the silence of the empty streets outside Dinham House was broken. An angry mob came surging down the road, marching either side of a wooden cart on which stood an enormous effigy of Napoleon Bonaparte, complete with his distinctive admiral's hat. Their voices grew louder, hurling insults and roaring at the tops of their voices for "Bony's brother" to come out of his house. Their faces were contorted with hatred. They thumped the air with their fists and brandished flaming torches above their heads. To Annie, looking down upon them from the window of the attic room where she had been trying to sleep, it seemed they were no longer Ludlow faces that she could recognise but one single slow-moving monster, a dragon breathing fire.

The procession drew up outside the gates of Dinham House.

"Come outside, Bony, come out," they chanted. The din brought Lucien and all the men in the house to the door. As soon as they saw him, the rioters pushed their torches into the bales of hay in the cart. Immediately the effigy of Napoleon took light. An enormous flame shot heavenwards. The shocked faces of Lucien and his household were suddenly lit up by the bonfire of his brother's likeness. Invisible to everyone else at the scene, Annie looked down on the flaming cart, the blazing straw-filled figure and the thick plume of black smoke which rose up from it. The crowd seethed around the entrance to the house. She could hear them jeering and laughing. A couple of young men tried to climb over the gates but were beaten back by Lucien's servants.

They are going to burn the house down with me and everybody else in it, she thought.

The sergeant-at-arms was slow in arriving and the crowd had dispersed. Not a single arrest was made that night.

Everything changed after that. You could have cut the atmosphere in the house with a knife. The music room concerts came to an abrupt stop. There were no more invitations to dinner, no more games of cards for the ladies. Lucien dismissed the English cook and would eat only food prepared by his own French chef. His suspicion was infectious. Alexandrine became fearful and withdrawn and pestered her husband every day to ask Lord Powis when they could leave Ludlow for the larger house he had promised them. As the Bonapartes became unhappier, Mrs Stringer became more tyrannical and made Annie's life a misery.

One morning, Christine-Egypta came in to the nursery where Annie was helping one of the French maids give breakfast to Paul-Marie and his little sister, Letitia. Annie wiped the baby's mouth with his bib and smiled, pleased to see a friendly face.

"You can go now, Annie Spears," Christine-Egypta said coldly, without even looking directly at her. "Brigitte can give them their breakfast by herself. Papa says you are not to come upstairs again."

Her cheeks burning with embarrassment, Annie took herself downstairs to the basement. Was she never going to hear a friendly word or see a smiling face ever again?

One morning a week or so after the burning of the effigy, Annie crept silently out of her attic bedroom and made her way down to work. It was still quite dark and only she and the other servants were about. A maid came panting up the stairs with a large lump of red-hot coal from the kitchen hearth to reset the fires in the bedrooms and public rooms. In the kitchen, Mrs Stringer was kneeling on the floor, riddling the ashes of the stove and gently squeezing the bellows to get the oven hot enough to bake the breakfast bread. Arthur was polishing a pair of men's riding boots for Lucien, who was in the habit of going out for an early morning ride with an English officer before the rest of the town was up and about.

"Annie Spears," said the housekeeper, as soon as she appeared in the kitchen shortly after six o'clock, "it's about time you got yourself down here. Draw half a dozen buckets of water and put the pans on to boil for the water jugs. Make sure you wait until it is good and hot, mind, or the men will be complaining they cannot shave."

Annie dragged herself off to the well-room to fetch the water. She had slept badly and was so tired she felt she might be sick. All night she had been tormented by dreams of buildings burning down and the grotesque figure of Napoleon being set alight. The memories of her mother and little sister were so painful she had to shut her eyes to stop thinking of them. As she cranked up the wooden bucket to fill it with water, she was thinking of William and wondering if she dared ask Mrs Stringer to let her go round to Quality Square and see him. It was ages since she had seen Sam too, and she hoped William might know how he had fared since the Frenchman found him in the shed. Surely he would not have run away from Ludlow without coming to say goodbye to her.

She carefully set down the full bucket of water on the floor and lowered another into the deep well. There was something about Sam that bothered her, something important nagging away at her brain. She had even been dreaming about him earlier that morning when Mrs Stringer banged on her door and startled her out of her sleep, but, try as she might, she could not remember what the dream had been about.

The tray and silver cutlery. The blood drained from Annie's face. That was what she had been dreaming about. She had clean forgotten to go and get the silver tray that she had used to carry Sam's supper out to the shed the night he had run away, the night her mother and Libby had been killed. She would have to go and get them and put them back in the pantry. If anyone else came across them, they might think Sam had stolen and hidden the lot until he could come back and get them. He was in enough trouble without being accused of being a thief.

Annie hauled up the last bucket of water and carried it into the kitchen. Mrs Stringer had her back to her, busy tapping the bottoms of the bread rolls to see if they were fully baked. Arthur's boot brushes and cloths still lay on the table where he had been working but the boots were gone. There was nobody else around.

She tiptoed out before anyone could shout an order at her and quietly crept up the back stairs to the yard. The top half of the stable-door was open and one of the grey carriage-horses stuck its head out and watched her as she scurried across the yard. She pulled back the stiff bolt of the shed door and went inside, drawing the door closed behind her. The shed was dark as pitch and smelled damp and unpleasant like any room that has been shut up for a long time. She wrinkled her nose and peered into the blackness. When her eyes had grown more accustomed to the dark, she began to feel her way around, steering a passage around all the stuff that had found its last home in the shed. There were piles of old furniture, chairs with sagging bottoms and tufts of horsehair spilling out of them, wooden boxes full of door handles, coils of rope, a stack of garden rakes and spades, something that might have been a yoke for an ox.

In one corner, against the wall, she came across a pile of cushions and fraying curtains that had probably belonged to an old coach. This would have been Sam's little nest, she thought. She slipped her hand under the cloth and immediately pulled it out again when it brushed against something bony. Gingerly, she lifted up the cloths and felt around again. It was the remains of the chicken leg that Sam had had for his supper weeks earlier. Beside it, she found the tray, the silver cutlery and the wine glass. She popped the cutlery and glass in her apron pocket, tucked the tray under her arm and darted out of the shed.

She hadn't gone more than a few yards across the yard when the horse gave a loud warning whinny. The noise made her jump and she let the silver tray clatter noisily to the ground where it skeetered off across the cobbled courtyard. As luck would have it, it came to rest against the door jamb of the coach-house just as Arthur the footman and a uniformed army officer came out leading two saddled horses. Lucien Bonaparte, sleek and handsome in full riding gear, followed behind them.

Arthur stooped down to pick up the tray. He saw Annie's terrified face but could do nothing to help her.

"What are you doing outside, girl?" demanded the officer.

Annie could not speak. She stood frozen to the spot in the middle of the yard.

"No harm done, sir. Just an accident, sir," Arthur began but the officer would not let the matter rest there. He walked forward, took the tray from Arthur's hand and examined it closely.

"It is a fine silver tray, I have to agree, with the Powis crest upon it. What is your name, girl?"

"Annie Spears, please, sir."

"Well, Spears, perhaps you would like to explain to us what you are doing carrying a silver tray outside at first light? Even King George's horses at Windsor do not have their oats served up in such style." He bent down and tilted up Annie's face so that her eyes directly met his. She was so frightened she could not think of anything to say. The officer repeated his question and shook her lightly by the shoulder.

"Thieving is a hanging offence, as well you must know. Did you think you could get away with it, eh?"

Annie shook her head miserably. Facing her, Lucien Bonaparte stood impassively looking on, striking his horse-whip gently against the side of his boot as if bored by the whole affair and anxious to leave for his morning ride.

"What else have you got?" demanded the officer.

Annie put her hand in her deep apron pocket and pulled out the silver knife and fork, the crystal goblet. "I wasn't stealing them. I was putting them back."

Arthur closed his eyes in dismay.

"Hold my horse, Arthur." The officer passed his horse's reins to the footman and seized Annie roughly by the shoulder. "By God, girl, you will regret this. I shall send for the sergeant-at-arms at once."

Lucien Bonaparte swung himself into the saddle of his grey mare. "Is it necessary to miss our morning ride for the sake of a petty thief? In another hour, the market square will be full of folk, and God knows, I don't want to see them any more than they wish to see me. It will only provoke more unpleasantness. Come, Lieutenant-Colonel, Arthur will keep the girl in his custody until we return."

He turned his horse towards the gate. The other horse which Arthur was holding tightly on a short rein pulled away hard and tried to follow it. Its hooves slipped on the wet cobbles.

"Whoa, there, girl," said Arthur.

The officer was torn between his duty to escort Lucien and his responsibility to deal with the thieving servant. The horses snorted nervously. Arthur, seeing that he was dithering, held out the reins.

"Do not let her out of your sight," the lieutenant-colonel warned, stepping on to the stirrup and swinging himself on to his saddle. "Keep her secure till I return. We shall soon get to the bottom of this affair."

"You are done for now, Annie," Arthur said as soon as they were gone. "Why did you take those things?"

Annie told the sorry story in between sobs as Arthur led her up the front steps and into one of the small parlours at the back of the house.

"It would have been better to have left the silver in the shed there to rot, but it is of no matter now for the harm is done."

"What will happen to me, Arthur?"

"I will be honest with you, Annie, so that you understand the trouble you are in. Your father is a transported convict, and you have no family here to put your case. When the sergeant-at-arms sees who you are, he will have you down for a felon like your father, no matter what you say."

"They will throw me in jail?"

Arthur looked long and hard at Annie's tear-streaked face. "Worse than that. If they caught you, you could end up swinging at the end of a rope in Shrewsbury Jailhouse. So," he said quickly, grabbing hold of Annie for her face had turned so white he was afraid she might faint, "I'll help you get away. You are lucky that Lucien needs an escort when he goes for his morning canter or the officer would have dealt with this himself."

He walked over to the window and looked down towards the river and the common. In the far distance he could see Lucien and the officer galloping over the linney. "He'll send for the sergeant-at-arms as soon as they return from their ride so we don't have much time. I'll show you where you can hide but you must leave Ludlow as soon as it grows dark. The townfolk are sure to raise a hue-and-cry to search for you once they know you have gone."

"But where shall I go? Where can I hide?" Annie grabbed hold of Arthur's hand. "God save me, Arthur, I

71

had better let them arrest me for I will never survive out there on my own. Let them hang me for my life is not worth living."

Arthur took both Annie's hands in his. "You will survive." He drew Annie over to the fire-place. "This is your only hope, Annie. Most of the chimneys in this house are connected," he explained. "If you climb this one, you will find a ledge on your right hand side. There is a narrow passage through to the other side, leading down into the fireplace in the music room. They haven't lit fires in there since the ladies stopped giving their afternoon concerts. Stay on the ledge until you hear the parish clock strike four o'clock this afternoon. You will hear the bells for I often used to hear them when I was a sweep. Come down into the music room then. I will leave a window a fraction open but you must take your chances after that."

"But I cannot climb a chimney. I do not know how to climb."

"It is your only chance. You must press your back against the chimney wall and push with your feet. Good luck, Annie Spears, and may God protect you."

"What about you? What will you say?" Annie asked.

"Don't worry about me. I will be all right. I will think of some explanation."

"Will you tell William what has happened?"

Arthur nodded, then turned sharply on his heel and left the room. Annie heard the door lock behind him. She looked up the empty black hole of the chimney, then stepped into the grate.

Chapter 8

William Spears was proud to be a hatter. In the two years that he had been apprenticed to Abraham Smart, he had watched and practised every one of the processes until he was almost as good as Abraham himself. He knew just how much fur or silk to measure out for a hat, how to bathe it in hot water, then roll and stretch it, steam it on the block, cut and shape and stitch the silk lining, add the trimmings, the buckles or bands. He had learnt every task, down to the final brushing that made the hat lustrous and shiny. It was hard work but better than most for the Smarts treated him fairly. He wished his father could see the fine silk top hat he had made for himself.

Mrs Smart was a hatter like her husband; she made ladies' silk bonnets trimmed with frills and long matching bow-ties and, by special commission, parasols of shot silk with carved ivory handles. The Smarts needed William for they had no children of their own – but they were far from sentimental about him. When his mother had been killed, they were happy to have him live in with them but stopped paying him his weekly wage. "It is for your own good, so that you may learn the value of money," Mrs Smart said. "Victuals cost money." Fortunately, Mr Smart was not as sensible as his wife and gave William the occasional tip of threepence or sixpence. "Wills," he said, "you play your cards right by me and I'll see you don't go short."

William did not easily trust people but he liked the mad hatter. Almost the worst thing in his life after the shock of learning that his father had been sent away to the farthest corner of the world was seeing how their friends and neighbours had treated them. Slowly but surely he had seen them shun his mother's company. His father's work-mates at the tannery crossed the road rather than speak to them. They did not care that his sisters, first Annie and then little Libby, were almost broken by the long hours of sewing gloves. D'arcy Haggitt, the headmaster of the grammar school, never missed an opportunity to remind the school assembly that William Spears was the son of a convict, a charity case whose fees were generously paid by the glover Mr Evans. William used to burn with anger and shame. He was ashamed of his father ashamed of being the son of a transported convict, no matter how often Kezia told him to love his father, and believe in his innocence. He had hated his mother for making little Libby work, keeping her awake until midnight, prodding her with a needle to stop her falling asleep. When he saw that she would rather have both Libby and Annie working than take charity from the parish, he had left school, saying that he had had enough of book-learning and would find a job. Evans had promptly put up the rent, leaving them no better off. Now both his mother and sister were dead and his heart was broken. He began to understand how that villain, Evans, had been manipulating Kezia, forcing her towards a marriage she did not want but perhaps felt she could not avoid. Above all, he felt guilty and confused. He wished he had loved his mother more. More than anything, he wished he could be with his father.

On the morning of Annie's capture at Dinham House, Abraham Smart and William were in the upper workshop setting up new blocks for Abraham's experimental collapsible opera hat when they heard a commotion coming from the market square around the corner.

"Sounds like some excitement in the town, Wills," said Abraham, looking over the top of his half-moon glasses. "Do you want to go and see if a felony has been committed?"

"If you say so, Mr Smart."

"I do say so, Wills, and you can run an errand for me at the same time. There are leather hat-boxes waiting for collection at the saddler's down Fish Lane. You fetch them, and Mrs Smart will be pleased to give you double helpings of pudding at dinner-time, won't you, my dear?"

He glanced over at Mrs Smart who was sitting at the window stitching a rich burgundy silk lining into an Easter bonnet that the glamorous American actress, Miss Brooks, had ordered. She did not even glance in their direction, but sighed loudly as if to suggest that pudding was the last thing on her mind. Her husband carefully removed two gold sovereigns from his waist-coat pocket and pressed them into William's hand. "Hold them tight in your pocket, William," he said, tapping the side of his nose with a long finger. "There may be thieves about."

A crowd of people were standing jeering in front of the town stocks as William rounded the corner. The bailiff was trying to fasten Israel Bessell, the sweep, into the leg and neck braces. Bessell was extremely drunk. His head lolled forward as if the muscles of his neck could no longer support its weight. His eyes rolled. His legs and arms thrashed the air uselessly. The bailiff could hardly keep him still long enough on the bench to lock him into place.

"And you can stay there until you sober up, you good-for-nothing scoundrel," said the bailiff, fastening down the last lock.

Bessell belched loudly.

"Cor, what a stink," someone shouted, holding their nose.

"Clean him up, then," shouted someone else, so, to great applause, a carter picked up a bucket of water that his donkey had been drinking out of and hurled it in Bessell's direction. The sweep growled like a dog, then let his head drop forward and promptly fell asleep.

As the crowd drifted away from the stocks, a party of militiamen marched into the square and drew up in front of the castle gates. The lieutenant colonel from Dinham was there and his sergeant-at-arms, shouting for the people to gather around. William forced his way through the crowd to hear what they were saying.

"What is going on?" he asked the man standing next to him. "Who are they talking about?"

"A servant from Dinham House has bolted, it appears. Annie Spears by name."

"Annie?" The blood drained from William's face. "What do they say she has done?"

"She was making off with some silver, as far as I can make out. They had placed her under house arrest but she made a run for it."

"It's not possible. Annie is no thief."

A hand grasped William's shoulder.

"This is the brother of the girl you seek, a right bad'un like his father, I expect," said Mr Evans in a loud voice for all the crowd to hear. "Perhaps he can tell us where she could be hiding."

William pulled away from him. "Let go of me. My sister has done no wrong. And I would not tell you where she was hiding even if she had robbed the mails."

He ducked down to wriggle free from Mr Evans' grip and tried to move away through the crowd.

"Stop that boy," cried Evans.

A pair of labourers who had just come into the square and so did not know why the crowds had collected, heard the glover's cry, saw William darting away, and jumped to the conclusion that he must be a pickpocket. They turned on their heels to chase after him and, like a pack of over-excited hounds following the call of the huntsman's bugle, the crowd in the square turned and followed them.

It was useless for William to stop, stand his ground and declare his innocence. He made off down a narrow lane at the corner of the square with the mob snapping at his heels. A horse and cart, almost as wide as the lane itself, was coming towards them. Frightened by the shouts of the men bearing down on it, the horse reared up, toppling the carter from his seat. William seized the chance to slip through the narrow gap. Then, in the darkness of the overhanging jetty of a tailor's shopfront, he caught a glimpse of royal blue livery, the costume of Napoleon's French servants. One of them stepped out to block his way. William ducked and weaved to get past into one of the even narrower alleys between the houses. Suddenly, there was a silver flash, the flick of a knife. William kicked out at his attacker. The knife flew up into the air and rattled over the cobbles. The first of the crowd to get past the horse behind him gasped. William ran on with the yells of his pursuers ringing in his ears. "Did you see the knife? That rascal pulled a knife."

He darted down an open doorway and into a passageway that led to the back of a house. Here there were more houses, a teeming warren of mean dilapidated slums and dismal yards with groups of ragged barefoot children squatting in the rubbish. He bolted past them, cleared a wall, came down near the town walls, fled under the arch and raced blindly on down towards the river. He shot across Ludford Bridge and into the woods of Whitcliffe. Only then did he realise that he could no longer hear the yells of the crowd. He had thrown them off. Panting with exhaustion, he sank down on to a large stone to catch his breath. On the opposite bank of the river, the castle and its steep forbidding walls loomed grimly over him.

William was greatly shocked by what had happened. Now he knew how the hare or the fox or the deer felt when it heard the barking of the hounds behind it. He had seen men and women, neighbours and traders that he saw every day, turn against him for no reason. Even if they realised they had made off after the wrong person, he was too frightened to go back yet. Anyone might point a finger at him and start the chase again. William knew that it was not only the guilty who were punished: his own father was as far from England as it was possible to be for a crime he had not committed. Now Annie was missing, accused of being a thief too – and the name Spears was enough for everyone to jump to conclusions. William was certain his sister could not have stolen anything – he would kill her himself if she had – but he had to find her and talk to her. Ludlow was no longer a safe place for either of them.

They would both have to run away, he thought, though he could not for the life of him think where they could go or how to travel, since they had neither money nor friends to help them. Rich folk could take the mail coach and reach London in a day-and-a-half, but what could outcast children do? It took about ten days to walk to the capital, people said, and that was if they could find their way and keep out of sight of the militia. He and

Annie would be worse than tramps, turned away and despised wherever they went. Towns were safe enough places for those who belonged to them but not for a pair of penniless orphans. He had seen the people of Ludlow staring suspiciously at strangers, had seen the bailiffs march beggars off to the jailhouse. It would be the same for them in other towns.

He looked down at the river Teme, at the water gliding over the weir beside the mill. All rivers flow to the sea, he remembered from his school days. Where did the Teme go? he wondered. If there was a boat moored somewhere along the bank, perhaps he and Annie could reach the sea. No, he thought unhappily, you cannot hide from people's prying eyes out on the middle of a river.

He wished there was someone he could trust, someone who would help them get away, but he could think of no one, not even Abraham Smart, the mad hatter, who would shield a thief from the law. Oh, what had Annie done to have got herself and himself into such trouble, he thought in exasperation. And where was she hiding?

Chapter 9

The chimney was a terrifying place. Wedged uncomfortably on the narrow ledge between the flues of the music room and the back parlour, Annie waited and listened to the sounds of the house. It was pitch black, a darkness that she had never known, for not a chink of daylight penetrated the chimney linings. It was not like that darkness of a room in the middle of the night when shapes and shadows gradually begin to make sense. She could see nothing. This was the darkness of the grave, Annie thought, and just as cold. The soot caught the back of her throat but she dared not so much as cough or clear her throat for fear someone in one of the rooms below should hear her. Every sound was magnified. She heard the bells of the parish church ring out every hour as Arthur had told her but she also heard footsteps running up and down the staircases, doors being flung open and closed, the raised voices of the servants and soldiers as they searched the house for her. She could hear little Paul-Marie crying, and wished someone would go and comfort him. All day carriages came and went.

Once she heard someone entering the music room and thought her heart would stop with fright. She prayed it was not one of the maids come to light a fire, but whoever it was drew up a seat in front of the spinet and lazily picked out a few notes of a dance tune. She could hardly believe they could not hear her breathing and the thumping of her heart, and had almost made up her mind to come tumbling down into the hearth and give herself up except that the very thought of moving terrified her even more than fear of the gallows. The climb up to the ledge, pushing her back against the chimney wall and levering herself upwards with her feet, had worn her out. Her ankles, knees, shoulders, felt skinned and bloody. To go down again was certain to be hell. She truly wished she were dead. The hours seemed interminable.

But when the parish church bells at last rang out four o'clock in the afternoon, she knew she must do what Arthur had told her. She braced her feet and back against the chimney wall and began the slow careful descent down the black hole into the music room, inch by painful inch, fearful that every scraping of her shoes, every laboured breath would bring someone scurrying into the room. At last, when she thought her strength would give out, her feet jammed against the iron hand-holds just above the widening mouth of the ingle-nook fireplace. She looked down and saw the light coming up from the room. She gratefully let herself slide down the last few remaining feet.

Blinking away the soot that covered her eyes and face, she ran to the window as Arthur had told her to. It was a sash window, a modern style, not like the casement windows of the older houses that opened outwards. Panicking, she pushed and pulled at it with her black hands, terrified that she would never get it open, until she realised she had to push it up. It slid noiselessly upwards on its sash. Annie slipped over the ledge and dropped down, gasping in the sweet fresh air.

As her feet reached the ground, a hand closed over her mouth and something dark and heavy was flung around her shoulders. She was half-carried, half dragged away from the house. Too weak to resist, she let herself fall limply into her captor's arms.

"Come on, Annie," hissed a voice in her ear. "Don't make it any more difficult for me than you have to. Walk properly – and don't make a sound." It was Arthur.

Annie's mind raced with a thousand questions. Why was Arthur arresting her now after he had allowed her to hide all day? Where was he taking her? Who was he taking her to? But above all, why?

He bundled her through the gates and under an archway into the castle gardens. Darkness had already fallen so the ladies and gentlemen who liked to stroll there had long since gone home. There was not a soul to be seen.

"Right," he said, pushing a bundle into her arms, "I've brought you some food for your journey and your red cape. Wrap it tightly around you for you are trembling with the cold. It will keep you warm – and hide your dirty clothes from view for you have half the soot of Dinham on your dress and apron. Now the best way to go out of the town is . . ."

"You're not handing me back to the sergeant?" Annie whispered. Her voice after all the hours of silence came out as a croak.

"Of course not. Is that what you thought?" Arthur pushed her hair back from her face.

"Is everyone looking for me?"

"They *were* looking for you but now they think hunger and cold will drive you out of hiding. A reward has been offered for your capture – but I doubt anyone will earn it. For you, Annie Spears, will shortly be in Bristol."

"Bristol?" echoed Annie. The name meant nothing to her.

"I have a brother, David, who is an ostler at the inn where all the coaches stop. The Lamb and Flag. Tell him I sent you. He will help you find work."

"But how ever shall I get to Bristol? How far is it from here?"

"By a road no one will ever think of, so no one will follow you. By Offa's Dyke."

Annie frowned.

"It is like a wall, Annie, a high bank built of earth by an ancient king long ago," explained Arthur. "It stretches from one end of Wales right to the other. All you have to do is follow the wall south, keeping high up on the hills and ridges, with Wales on your right and England on your left until you come down to the sea."

Annie stared at him, confused and frightened. She knew nothing about the sea or travelling on hills and mountains. There might be wolves. "But, Arthur, where will I find this wall? And how long must I walk?"

"At Knighton," he said, mentioning a small town a dozen miles from Ludlow, right on the border with Wales. "Four days' walking from there will get you to the sea, I reckon."

"Four days?" Annie was shaking from head to toe with fear and panic.

Arthur nodded.

"I had rather give myself up to the sergeant-at-arms and let myself rot in jail than climb mountains for four days, all alone." Tears rolled down her face.

"But you will not be alone," said Arthur. "William will take you."

"William? Is he here?" Annie sniffed and wiped her nose on the back of her sleeve.

"I found him up hiding in the shepherd's hut earlier and told him what happened."

"William was hiding? Why?"

"He'll tell you the whole story himself when you see him. He is waiting for you now at the bottom of Corve Street by the bridge. God go with you both and bring you good luck." Arthur hugged her closely to him. "Be brave, Annie, and soon this will all be behind you. Now go quickly before we are seen together."

Annie followed the path through the trees around the outside of the castle walls. She rushed headlong along the broad linney and down the old lane behind the churchyard where her mother and sister lay in their cold graves. As she came around the corner to the bridge across the river, a carriage went by but the driver did not give her a second glance. She could smell the unmistakable throat-tightening smell of the tannery yards by the river, that smell of leather that she had grown up with. A couple of men walked past her on the other side of the street. She recognised them, men who worked in the tanneries just a few hundred yards from her old burnt-out home, but they hurried past her as if she was a ghost, too taken up with their own conversation to pay attention to a small girl carrying a bundle of cloths.

This was the very edge of the town. Beyond it lay open countryside, and a road leading to places she had never been for she had never been further from home than the meadows down by the riverbank where she used to play with William and Libby on summer afternoons. She crossed the bridge, looking to right and left for any sign of her brother. A sheep in the field alongside her watched her and bleated inquisitively.

Where was William? And why was he not waiting for her? In the corner of her eye, she fancied someone or something moved. There was a flash, a dark shape scurrying past but when she turned back she saw nothing but the humpy uneven tussocks of grass and a few ewes huddled for comfort together by the hedge.

"William," she called out in a low whisper.

There was no answer but, from in among the sheep, a figure stood up, a small boy wearing a top hat.

"Hello, Annie," said Sam Price, "Give us a hand up. I've run away again and this time, it's for good."

"So have I," said Annie, "and so has William, I think."

At that moment, there was a whistle from the other side of the bridge and William came running towards them.

Chapter 10

That first night was long and hard for the three runaways. They left the town behind them and walked for hours along the old cattle drovers' road in the direction of Knighton. At first Sam whined and whinged, complaining that the others were going too fast for him, but when William made it clear he must keep up or fall back on his own, he eventually stopped moaning. They plodded on, saving all their energy for placing one foot after another, never once stopping until they had left Ludlow well behind them. They crept around sleeping hamlets and the brooding shadows of churches, taking fright at every rustling in the ditches and every barking dog, but they need not have worried. In the cover of darkness, they had the whole countryside to themselves for every honest soul in the county was fast asleep in bed, and nothing moved except prowling foxes and snuffling badgers.

The worst thing, more than the cold biting wind, the pain in every limb and the hunger, was the fear that drove them on. Once William stopped and said to Annie, "Did you do it?"

"No!" she answered, shrinking back from him for she thought he was going to hit her. "I had forgotten the tray I brought out to Sam weeks ago, the day he first ran away."

"Oh," said Sam, laying both his hands on his tummy, "what a feast that was, chicken and cheese and . . ."

"So," interrupted William, "you stole the food?"

"Yes," agreed Annie, "but Sam hadn't eaten all day. You were there when we hid him in the shed."

"That alone would be enough for them to get you," said William grimly. "And it's your word against theirs that you weren't going to pawn the tray. You know that with our father already branded a criminal we daren't put a foot wrong. How could you be so stupid? And why did you give Sam his food on a tray anyway?"

"Oh William, don't you see," Annie said, "it was easier to walk out of the kitchen with food all set out on a tray than with my apron pockets stuffed."

They walked on in silence until Sam's voice piped up in the darkness.

"There was a woman from Diddlebury that was hanged for taking flax that was lying bleaching in a field." He sniffed. "And another boy from Clee Hill that was transported to Botany Bay for taking a snuff-box and an umbrella from the vicar's house."

Annie gasped. There was a loud groan as William's boot shot out and caught Sam's shin. Nobody spoke again, though Sam slipped his hand consolingly into Annie's.

They trudged on through the darkness until they came to the milestone which told them Knighton was only one mile away. Ahead of them rearing up into the night sky were the stark outlines of the Welsh mountains. The town clock showed a quarter to midnight.

"We'll stop here," said William, "for I shan't be able to make out the dyke until it's light." The sight of the mountains had shaken him. When Arthur had told him about Offa's Dyke, it had all seemed so easy, but now he was afraid he would never be able to recognise it. He looked at Annie who was gingerly examining the blisters on her ankles, and at Sam, shivering in his filthy thin ragged jacket. How would he ever find the trail and get them safely to the sea? They looked back at him with peaky frightened expressions.

"Cheer up," he said, forcing himself to smile, "let's find somewhere to shelter and have a bite to eat."

There was a broken-down barn outside the town limits. Part of its roof had fallen in and the door was hanging off its hinges. The three children looked in at the bare filthy floor. It did not look very comfortable.

"Well," said Sam, at last, kicking a heap of dirty rags out of his way, "I've slept in worse places, I can tell you, and then got kicked out of them to climb chimneys. I am never ever going to do that again. This is good enough for me."

They slept fitfully there that night, all three waking at the slightest sound. The damp floor made Sam cough. Annie tossed and turned and made little whimpering noises as she dreamed. William fought with his conscience. As he had lain down on the ground, a chink from his trouser pocket had reminded him that he still had Abraham Smart's two gold sovereigns. That made him a thief in the eyes of the law too. He knew he should tell Annie but he was too embarrassed and besides, he wanted her to suffer a little longer for forcing them both into flight from Ludlow. He would never be a hatter now, would never see the name *Spears* written on the sign-post that swung out over the cobbles of Quality Square.

Before the first cock crowed, the three were on their way again, creeping through the slumbering village. "At Knighton," Arthur had told William, "walk through the town up the main street, following the river – it's our river, you know, the Teme, same as here in Ludlow – then climb up the hill on the far side. Keep the town behind you and walk on."

William and Annie and Sam panted their way to the top of the hill.

"Is this the dyke?" asked Sam, pointing at every bump in the ground. "Is this it?"

William shook his head. He had bitten his lip so hard, it had begun to bleed. He scanned the hills, not really sure what he was looking for. Annie pointed at the same time as he did.

King Offa's Dyke was like a massive bank of earth, anything from ten to twenty feet high, with a wide ditch running to one side of it. It wound across the countryside like a huge grass snake that constantly changed direction. It strode across hills and valleys, climbed up hills and followed the tops of ridges where long ago the ancient rulers of Mercia had kept watch against the marauding Welsh. In places it was wooded and the three children had to pass through damp dripping forests, where every shadow and every sound frightened them. They walked swiftly, hardly speaking at all as the enormity of what they were doing hit them. They were runaways now, and labelled thieves and troublemakers into the bargain. There was no going back. William and Annie constantly looked over their shoulders, imagining the sound of horses' hooves or the distant holler of trackers bearing down on them. Sam shuffled along beside them, chatting cheerfully when the going was easy about how he was going to see the world, and panting grimly up the steep hills.

About four hours after they had left Knighton, after a long climb, they came down into the valley of a river. The river was flowing very fast, swollen from the melting snows of winter. In places, the banks were badly flooded. Flocks of upended ducks fished for food in what should have been meadows and a swan glided past them, jabbing at her back feathers with her beak like a woman poking at uncomfortable corsets.

They sat down on a wooden footbridge in the watery sunshine and divided out the rest of the pie and cheese that Arthur had put in Annie's bundle.

"How did you know I was on the run? Was it Arthur who told you?" Annie asked.

"No, I heard about it in the square. The sergeant was calling for people to help hunt you down. Evans set the crowd after me. I had to run away."

Sam laughed and flung a bit of cheese at the ducks. "Then how did you know where to find Annie?"

"Arthur told me. When he heard that the crowd had gone after me, he guessed I would go up and lie low in the old shepherd's hut. He followed me up there and told me to meet you at the bridge after dark." William clammed up abruptly. He still could not bring himself to talk about the gold sovereigns which burned like hot coals in his jacket pocket.

"Shall we make it, William?" Annie asked, after a while.

"Of course we shall. No one will think of looking for us up here. If they have gone after us, they will be out searching on the London road. I even said as much to Mrs Stringer the day at the graveyard. I told her we'd rather run to London than be put in the workhouse."

"Do we have to go much farther before we stop for the night?" said Sam, throwing a piece of pie crust over to the swan.

"It's no use asking me. I've never been here before. We'll walk until night falls. And stop throwing away good food," he added, reaching out and grabbing Sam's wrist. "You don't know where your next meal is coming from. It could be four days before we reach Bristol."

"William," said Annie, "what shall we do when we get there? Won't they still be after us?"

William looked sharply at his sister. "In Bristol we will be three among many thousands," he answered. "Arthur's brother will help us to find work. You can work in a dressmaker's, or as a servant in an inn."

"And what will you do, William?"

"Work for a hatter perhaps or, if I can't find one to take me on, I shall take a job in a tanner's like father used to do. We'll find something. We'll stick together."

Sam stood up and stretched. He threw one last crumb to the swan before William could stop him. "There are ships in Bristol," he said, his eyes shining bright with excitement, "ships that go all over the world. Whaling ships." He grinned at Annie. "I'm bound for the South Seas."

"Then, come on," said William, setting his top hat on his head, "let's get on our way before the Shropshire militia catch up on us."

After that, the path climbed steeply again. All afternoon they stayed up high, giving the villages in the valleys a wide berth and steering clear of any isolated farm-houses for fear someone might spot them and set a search party on their trail. Occasionally they heard the warning barking of a dog or saw one running in the fields below but none came near. As the afternoon went on, the sky clouded over and the day grew darker. The wind was cutting through their clothes, chilling them to the bone. Flakes of snow drifted in from the Welsh side of the dyke and settled on their hair and shoulders. There was no shelter to be had anywhere. Sam and Annie were already dragging their feet, lagging a hundred yards or more behind William. They looked worn out, with sad pinched white faces, all the spirit drained out of them. They would not last the night out in the open, he knew. From further down the valley, he heard a church bell toll six o'clock and, squinting hard, fancied he saw the distant lights of a small village. It was impossible to know whether it was safe or not but, at the very least, they might find shelter for the night again in some old barn. He called to his sister and Sam to catch up.

"Listen," he said when they arrived panting and wheezing beside him. "We'll take shelter down there for the night."

They came down the side of the hill, following the path of a little brook. Soon they could see the road into the village and the bobbing lantern of a carter trotting along on his waggon. A woman's sing-song voice cried out "chooky, chooky, chooky," as she called her chickens home for the night. At the narrow wooden bridge over the stream and into the main street, there was a milestone.

"Hay-on-Wye, fourteen miles," William read out slowly.

"But where are we now? What's the name of this place?" whispered Sam to Annie. "Are we even going in the right direction?"

Annie lifted her shoulders and let them drop. She was too cold to speak. They all looked down the long straight road, dark except for the yellow pools of light thrown out by the candles in the cottage windows. They cautiously crossed the bridge and tip-toed down the village street, careful to keep in to the shadows. The entire village seemed to consist of no more than a string of old thatched and timbered cottages along a dirt road, a church with a graveyard full of leaning tombstones and, at the very end, an inn with a sign showing a cow with a crumpled horn. It creaked on its hinges. A lantern was hanging outside the door but they could not hear any sign of life inside.

"Come on," whispered William. He crept around to the back of the inn. There was a rough yard at the back, and a stable block at right angles to the inn itself. The doors were closed and bolted – if there were horses inside, they had already been bedded down for the night. He slipped the bolt back as quietly as any burglar and beckoned to the others to follow quietly behind him.

The stable was long and narrow with stalls on either side. It smelled foul, of wet straw and manure and rising damp that almost made the three children gag when they entered. There were two old chestnut horses lying together in one of the stalls. Sam heard their breathing and clambered up to peer over the half-door: the poor bony beasts did not even move. They had been driven too long and too hard that day and were too worn out to object to sharing their stable. In the tack-room at the far end, there was a broken cart-wheel leaning up against the wall, some saddles hanging on nails and a few bales of straw, not as clean as they might have been, but dry enough to use as makeshift bedding.

"We can stay here," said William, "but we must leave long before dawn."

"What if someone comes?" asked Annie.

"Annie!" William snapped. "No one will come. Try to sleep."

But sleep did not come easily to either Annie or

William. The horses wheezed and snorted and banged their hooves against the fragile wooden partitions as they shifted in their sleep. The roofbeams creaked and groaned. The fear of capture and a return to Ludlow's jail – or worse – was harder to put aside than the pangs of hunger or the discomfort of the damp straw. The smell of the leather saddles reminded them of the tanned hides drying in the tanneries in Corve Street and the burnt-out shell of their home. They tossed and turned but did not speak to one another even though each knew the other was awake. Between them Sam lay stretched out. His hands were raised above his head with the fingers curled towards the centre of his palms like a baby without a care in the world. All Annie could think of was how soon they could get far away and back up to the safety of the dyke.

Some time later Annie must have dozed off for she suddenly came to with a start. It was still pitch dark in the windowless stable but outside a cock was crowing. Then another one further off up the valley answered it with an even more raucous din. She picked a long piece of straw from her hair and rubbed her eyes. Above her she could hear scratching sounds, and immediately thought of rats. Something brushed against her cheek. She looked up and made out the unmistakable shape of Sam in his top hat inching along the beam directly above her head. Almost at once, there was a violent squawking. An enraged hen flew down from her nest in the rafters and landed at her feet. Sam plopped down on to the straw beside her, his body dropping with the gentle thump of a fall of soot. He held open his cupped palms to show Annie three brown eggs.

"Come on," said William, seizing his hat, "let's get out of here before someone comes to see why the hens are in such foul temper."

It was a long hard trudge all that second day on the dyke. They tried hard not to be discouraged by the steep hills but just plodded on. One rocky ridge and peak followed the other. It was wild, lonely country with hardly a sign of life but for the flocks of black-faced mountain sheep and bleating newborn lambs. By early afternoon, they had descended into a wide river valley and saw the distant roofs and steeples of a town they thought must be Hay-on-Wye but were too nervous to go near. Besides, to the south loomed more mountains, blacker and higher than any they had seen in two days' walking, and they knew that their route lay in that direction.

Their path began to rise steeply, and even when they felt they must have reached the very top, the dyke would zig-zag around a corner and point them ever higher. Sam's breathing was bad. He had to stop more and more often to cough and splutter, bringing up gobbets of black soot-stained catarrh. Once far off they saw a team of drovers and a herd of cattle coming in their direction but before they had got much nearer they had suddenly veered off on the English side between two mountain peaks. Now and then, flurries of snowflakes swirled around them. It was becoming impossible to follow their course. In the half-light and with the earth all around them covered with a sprinkling of snow, William could not make out the distinctive shape of Offa's Dyke. Whole sections of it seemed to have disappeared altogether. The weather was closing in and seemed set to get much worse before it got better.

They began to make their way down the mountainside to take shelter in a small stand of trees. William, walking in front, suddenly stopped and put his hand to his ear. Somewhere nearby there was a distant knocking sound, the rhythmic sound of metal on stone like someone hammering. All three froze where they stood like wild animals who have scented danger, every nerve in their body primed to run. In the stillness, their eyes scanned the hills a few hundred yards above them. It was Sam who first spotted the solitary black-coated figure beyond the trees. He had his back to them and seemed to be standing hammering at the rock cliff. After a while, he stopped and closely examined whatever it was he held in his hand. Abruptly the strange figure turned, raised his arms to the heavens and began to sing at the top of his voice although the words were carried off by the wind.

"What on earth is he doing?" asked Annie.

"Who knows?" replied William, "but we'd best keep out of his way. He's a clergyman."

They crept further into the shadow of the trees. Deep in the centre of the wood, it was very still and a good deal warmer. It was almost as good as coming indoors after the chill of the wind and snow on the higher ground.

"I need to stop," said Sam, suddenly dropping down to

sit on the exposed roots of a tree. "I'm hungry and my feet are done in."

"Mine too," said Annie, pushing a finger down at the back of her tough leather boots to rub her heel. "I've got a new blister."

William looked at them both in exasperation. He was stronger than they were and would have preferred to press on but he knew the weather and the landscape were against them all, even if the little ones had not been so worn out. They would have to find shelter and rest up until the weather cleared.

"Wait there," he said. "Don't move." He pressed his finger against his lips, warning them not to call out after him, and walked off down through the trees. About twenty minutes later he was back.

"There's a ruined abbey down in the valley," he said. "We'll stop there tonight."

Sam and Annie followed him out of the little wood, and down into the valley towards the ruins of an old monastery. Its roof had fallen in almost entirely and its nave and side-chapels were overgrown with nettles, brambles and all variety of weeds, some of them waist-high. Free-standing stone pillars that once had supported the weight of the roof soared sixty feet up to the heavy snow-laden skies. Crumbling staircases led nowhere. Sam ran wildly through the arched doorways, climbed up on the sills of graceful vaulted windows and peered into the long deserted dovecote where centuries earlier monks had reared pigeons for their winter pies.

Annie stood still under the gaunt grey ruins,

convinced that there were eyes watching her, people ready to pounce the moment she let down her guard. There was a doorway opposite her. Its door had long since disappeared but the frame had been blocked up with piles of fallen masonry. As she watched, the twitching snout of a fox appeared at a gap at the bottom of the rubble. She stood stock still, the stillest thing for miles around. The fox nudged aside a stone, sniffed the air, came out from under cover, then, too late, spotted her. Their eyes met for a moment and then it was off, running like a demon out of the ruins and across the meadow to the hill beyond.

Annie knelt down and peered into the hole where the fox had emerged. There was another room behind and, dimly visible behind a round column, she could see a flight of stairs leading down underground.

"William," she called. "Come and see."

With bare hands so cold they were almost too numb to feel the pain, all three cleared a hole big enough to crawl through into the room behind. The steps led down to the crypt, a low dark basement whose walls felt damp and clammy to the touch, but the floor was dry and at least its roof provided shelter from the wind and sleet. They bedded down for their third night on the run, carrying down armfuls of bracken to lay on the floor, but it was hardly more comfortable than the night in the stable. The crypt was draughty and Annie, unable to sleep, lay petrified, listening to the patter of small feet criss-crossing the floor and the eerie screams of owls as they glided under the abandoned stone archways. She felt hungry, homeless and friendless and secretly wished they had never set out on this adventure. She could hear William tossing about and knew he was awake and thinking too. Sam's breathing was deep and even as a baby's.

"We can't go on like this, William," she said. "It's worse than being a wild animal. Perhaps we should give ourselves up."

"No! They have you down for a thief, Annie, don't you understand? You wouldn't be put in the workhouse. They could hang you like they were going to hang father. And Bessell would whip Sam within an inch of his life if he laid hands on him again."

"I told you. I'm going to sea," said Sam quietly in the darkness. "I shan't ever give myself up."

"I'm afraid, William," said Annie.

"I'm just hungry," said Sam. "I can't think of anything but my empty belly."

"Tomorrow I shall get us something to eat," William said. He thought of the two gold sovereigns tucked away at the bottom of his coat pocket but once again let the moment pass without telling Annie and Sam his guilty secret.

Chapter 11

"More gravy, Mr Lewis?"

"Thank you, Dai, I don't mind if I do."

The Reverend Charles Lewis raised his knife and fork clear of his plate so that the innkeeper's young servant could pour more gravy over his Welsh mutton and potato pie. In the dining-room of the Bear and Ragged Staff in Hay, he could always count on a good dinner after a cold and exhausting ride down the mountains.

The Reverend Lewis was the curate of several small and impoverished parishes, not that he spent very much time attending to his duties in any of them. His passion was geology. It was the coming thing, he told anyone who would listen to him, for he could see that the crust of the earth held remarkable secrets, not just coal and gold and diamonds that could be mined, but fossils that made him question the whole of God's creation. Only that afternoon, he had come across an exposed rockface on which he could clearly make out the fossilised remains of hundreds of little fishes, bivalves and molluscs. This cold mountainy land had once lain beneath the sea. He had spent hours making exquisitely detailed drawings of feathery fins, and delicate lacy edged scallops, set in stone more than five million years ago. Now as he ate his dinner, he kept glancing down at his notebook and wishing he had someone to talk to.

At the corner table, between the window overlooking the street and the door into the kitchen, Oliver Waring, the eldest son of the workhouse master at Ludlow, huffily observed the preferential treatment the clergyman was getting. He scraped his chair back and smartly banged the salt cellar on the table to attract the waiter's attention.

The Reverend Lewis glanced over at him and politely nodded his head. He was a very thin man with a small bald head and a long delicate neck sticking up out of its collar, so that he looked a bit like an inquisitive, short-sighted and good-natured tortoise.

"A feast worth waiting for, I assure you," he said to the young man, waving a forkful of food at him. "You cannot fault Mrs Knill's mutton pie."

"That is why there is none left, no doubt. I am to be served the boiled beef."

The clergyman ignored the young man's surly tone. "An excellent choice, the beef is always excellent. Are you staying in the inn tonight?"

Mr Waring agreed that he was and looked impatiently towards the kitchen door.

"Then perhaps you would like to share my table and have a glass of claret with me while you are waiting," suggested the clergyman, expansively pointing at his bottle of wine and beckoning the other man to come and sit down beside him.

"That is very decent of you indeed," said Mr Waring, softening up at the prospect of a drink he would not have to pay for himself. "I would be delighted to join you."

The Reverend Lewis poured out two brimming glasses of claret. He coyly slipped his notebook in the other man's direction, laying it open at a faultless illustration of a section of the fossil beds he had been examining that afternoon. Mr Waring swallowed half his wine and replaced his glass on the open page, leaving a deep purple scar. The clergyman looked at his companion's chapped hands, his blunt nails which were none too clean, his fraying collar and greasy jacket. He was disappointed not to have a more educated companion to share his wine with.

"Are you travelling through?" he asked.

Mr Waring lowered his voice and looked around the empty dining-room.

"To tell you the truth, I have come from Ludlow, on a mission to hunt down some runaways. Bad'uns."

"Convicts?" The Reverend Lewis took a large pinch of snuff from his snuff-box, laid it out carefully on the side of his hand above his thumb and noisily sniffed it up each nostril in turn. "What or whom are they running away from?"

"It's two children I am after, a sister and brother by the name of Spears. The girl escaped house arrest after stealing silver plate from Lord Powis' house. And to make matters worse, her brother, trying to draw off the crowds who were after her, drew a knife upon a servant of Lucien Bonaparte's and made off with two sovereigns belonging to a hatter in the town. They must be caught before they do more mischief." The young man sat back, pleased that he had managed to mention both a Bonaparte and a lord of the realm in one breath.

"By God, man, they sound like an evil pair. I would not have thought children capable of such deception."

"Indeed they are," Waring lowered his voice. "It's their blood you see. Their father is already in Botany Bay – need I say more?" He threw his head back and drained the second half of his glass. "Have you seen any children travelling alone?"

"Not that pair, I am glad to say. I did see some children up in the woods this afternoon, close by the ruined priory at Llanthony, but there were three of them. I took them for the children of a sheep farmer, doubtless looking for a lost ewe. You would not credit how the hills are littered with lambing ewes this spring."

"Three children, you say? Not two? Could you describe them to me?"

"Why, sir, they were children," the Rev. Lewis pursed his lips. He would have found it easier to describe a fossil, an orchid, even a butterfly. He did not tend to look much at children. "There were three," he repeated, poking his head out further from his collar so that even the unimaginative Mr Waring found himself in mind of a tortoise, "two boys and a girl: an older boy, a girl half a head shorter, a smaller lad. More than that I cannot tell for I was at some distance from them and the light was fading. I only remarked on them because the two fellows were wearing top hats, an odd apparel I thought for country boys."

Oliver Waring rubbed his hands together and stood up.

"Those will be the very children I am after. I am much obliged to you, sir. The boy, William, was apprenticed to a hatter in the town."

"Come, come," said Mr Lewis, reasonably, "that is hardly cause to abandon your supper. Doesn't every man and boy wear a tall hat? If the possession of a hat was your only evidence, I fear you would be chasing after half the population of the country."

"You say, the little boy also wore a tall hat?"

"He did, a hat half as big as himself so that he looked like one of those children that sweeps have to put up chimneys."

"Sam Price, as I live and breathe!" Oliver Waring sucked his teeth. "So that is the third member of the party."

"Another Ludlow runaway?" The Rev. Mr Lewis raised an eyebrow.

"Aye, one whose master spent all of Tuesday in the town stocks for drunkenness and disorderliness. The boy would have had time enough and the opportunity to make a run for it." He looked impatiently at his watch as if he had already spent too much time talking and shouted for coffee.

"If they are the children you are seeking," the

clergyman said sadly, closing his wine-stained notebook, "they will have taken shelter for the night and in the darkness you will miss all trace of them. Wait till first light. I shouldn't think they could hide for ever in the Black Mountains."

Chapter 12

In the morning, before it was truly light, William, Annie and Sam crept out of the crypt and drew in their breath with astonishment at how beautiful the world appeared. It had not snowed any more during the night but there had been a hard frost and every blade of grass, every branch and twig, every soaring arch and pillar of the ruined priory stood out white in the cold air. Delicate white veins of frost spread out along the stony floor of the old church. They crunched beneath their feet. William tapped at the frozen water which had collected in a broken water-font and gave Sam and Annie a sliver of ice to suck. It was so cold it made their throats numb and their lips turn white and bloodless.

The shallow pools of floodwater on the grass beside the stream had completely frozen over. On one, a duck slithered and slipped, its webbed feet sliding all over the place like a tipsy skater. Sam stepped warily on to the ice, testing his weight with one foot, then holding one leg behind the other knee as if he would be lighter like that. The ice held firm. He slid off, laughing.

Annie joined him, catching his hand and letting him slide her along the frozen sheet of ice, shrieking and laughing with mock fear as it shifted and splintered a little but did not crack. Even William forgot for a few moments to worry. He smiled at Annie's happy face, took her by one hand, Sam by the other and the three of them spun around in a circle, faster and faster, the two boys in their black top hats, the girl in the middle like a red spinning top with her cape spreading out all around her.

It was Annie who saw Oliver Waring and the mounted militiamen riding towards them. She screamed out but the boys kept on spinning and laughing until she finally wrested her hands from theirs and broke the circle. William and Sam lost their balance and flew backwards. They turned to see what Annie was pointing at. The galloping horses bore down on them, their iron hooves shattering the crisp white stillness of the valley.

There was nowhere to run. The four horsemen surrounded them and the triumphant Mr Waring shouted, "Stand your ground, William Spears."

Like lambs to the slaughter, their hands were tied and they were taken back by road to Hay-on-Wye, Annie riding pillion on the captain's horse and Sam and William tied by rope and walking alongside until, exasperated by the slow pace they were making, the soliders hoisted the boys on to the backs of the horses too. So they were led into the town and up the hilly streets with jeering faces and pointing fingers following them until they finally arrived at the stable-yard of the Bear and Ragged Staff inn. A clergyman was standing by the mounting-block, waiting for a boy to finish saddling up his mare. He watched the sorry procession and shook his head sadly but said nothing.

Mrs Knill, the landlord, like many country innkeepers, had a room with barred windows where the watchman kept local wrongdoers, mostly poachers or sheep-stealers, until they could be taken to jail. William, Annie and Sam were thrown roughly into it and the key turned in the lock.

Nobody came to speak to them all morning and, shocked and terrified, they did not dare talk either but sat on the floor waiting for something to happen. Around mid-day, the door opened a fraction and a boy with terrified darting eyes pushed in a plate with three penny loaves and three tins full of teak-coloured tea.

"At least they are not going to starve us to death," said Sam, handing around the food to the other two who had not moved.

"What will happen to us, William?" whispered Annie.

William shoulders began to shake. "If only I had gone back with the money," he said between sobs.

"What money?" asked Annie.

"These," said William, drawing the two gold sovereigns out of his pocket and flinging them down on the floor.

Annie and Sam stared at the coins, bewildered.

"Where did you get them?" asked Annie.

"Mr Smart gave them to me to pay for the hat-boxes. I

didn't mean to steal them but I never went back, you see. We're all of us done for now."

"But nobody knows about them. You can hide them here or throw them out that window there. Nobody will be any the wiser," said Sam.

"It's no use. Mr Smart will have told them he had given me money to pay for the hat boxes. He probably thinks that is why I ran away," said William, ashamed and heartbroken that the mad hatter would think him so ungrateful.

"You called me stupid," said Annie in a low hurt voice though her eyes were flashing with anger.

"I'm sorry, Annie." He looked away, unable to meet her eyes. "I didn't want to be in charge of you. When Arthur found me and told me to take you away, I didn't want to go. I didn't want to run and hide. I just wanted to stay in Ludlow and make hats like Abraham Smart."

Sam picked up his tea and went to sit apart from the others below the window.

"Oh God," he prayed, "let them not send me back to Ludlow and Master Bessell. I could not bear it."

Soon afterwards, the soldiers came. They tied the children together and took them out to an open horse-drawn cart standing in the yard. A small crowd had gathered and stared at them curiously.

"Where are you taking us?" Sam asked the captain.

"To Shrewsbury Jail to wait until the Assizes," he answered, hauling up the back of the cart and drawing the bolt across.

"And may God have mercy on your souls," said Mrs Knill, as they drew away.

Chapter 13

At Shrewsbury jailhouse Annie was separated from her brother and Sam. Her cell was little more than an overcrowded stinking room where the inmates slept on the hard, cold, damp floor. Spiders, rats and cockroaches infested the place and when the weather improved and the temperature began to climb, flies hatched in the open drains and swarmed and buzzed around their heads.

Annie was struck dumb with fear and repulsion. Nothing she had seen in her short hard life had prepared her for such a hovel. She kept her head down, looking out at the world from under hooded eyes, only speaking when someone spoke to her, only moving to bolt forward and grab her food rations when they came. Her companions were thieves, beggars and debtors for the most part. There was one old laundry-woman accused of stealing a shift petticoat and a lace napkin. She was losing her wits with worry and sat rocking on the floor, scratching at her scalp with gnarled rheumatic fingers.

Others had been picked up for vagrancy, for begging in the public streets, for giving short measures in the markets.

There was one murderer, a woman who had been accused of stabbing her husband. "I loved him once," she said, "or I thought I did, but I swear I will go merrily to Hell and will kill him again if I meet his ghost in Hades for he destroyed my life." The night before she was taken away to be hanged, she gave the jailkeeper all the money she still had to bring her ale from the prison tap-room, and shared it out among the inmates while the hangmen hammered at her gallows in the courtyard opposite.

From the start, one young woman, Molly Llewellyn, took pity on Annie and sat beside her. Molly was only a few years older than Annie but she had a baby, a tiny downy-haired thing barely three months old, whom she kept tightly wrapped beneath her shawl all day long as if terrified someone would come and take him away from her. She had got pregnant when she was working as a servant and had been flung out by her mistress. The parson had denounced her for her immoral behaviour.

"Then they picked me up for begging outside the church on Sunday. They threatened to put me in the stocks but what was I to do? I had nowhere to go, no money. I stole a gentleman's purse off him, but they caught me before I had a chance to spend any of it."

"What will they do to you?"

"I don't know. They're all against me, first for having the baby, then for begging, now thieving. But what could I do, Annie, what could I do? The master would have his way." She clutched the baby, kissing the top of his downy head.

Many of the women knew they were likely to be hanged if they were found guilty. There were more than two hundred crimes that were punishable by hanging, nearly all of them crimes against property. It was clear that English law-makers thought thieves and muggers and forgers of bank-notes a far greater threat than rapists or murderers. And those that they did not hang, they sent to Australia, a vast empty continent on the other side of the world. It was as far from England as it was possible to be, a land no European had even heard of until forty odd years earlier when Captain Cook first landed on it. Now it was nothing less than a dumping-ground, a remote jail for England's unwanted criminals.

To people like those women in Shrewsbury jail who had never travelled more than a few miles from the house where they were born, the very thought of exile was more frightening than death itself. Rumours and half-truths flew around the cell, even though talking like this terrified them and made them sick with worry.

"They say as many as half the transports die on the long sea journey."

"And nobody ever returns even if they do survive and work out their sentence, for they can't earn their passage back."

Every day the conversation in the cells was of little else but public hangings or prison ships, especially as the date set for the assizes drew closer. They were like cats unable to leave off scratching their old flea-bites. Annie had no choice but to listen to them for there was nowhere to hide and no peace in the overcrowded cell. She recoiled in horror as they recited their litanies of men and women whom they had seen hanged.

"I remember my mother taking me to see a public hanging when I was scarcely seven or eight years old. She said I was to remember what I had seen and live my life in fear of the Law," the old laundry-woman said. "I can see him still as if it was yesterday. He was a highwayman, William Dempster, that the law had been after for many a year, and he went up the steps as jaunty as a bridegroom, waving and joking up to the minute the hangman placed the noose over his head. There must have been hundreds of people there to cheer him over the drop."

"May God have mercy on him," said another, "and give us the strength to do the same rather than blubbering and protesting our innocence."

But I am innocent, thought Annie. Surely they cannot hang me.

"There was a woman from Bromfield transported at the last sessions for stealing two chickens worth four pence," said a woman who had stolen enough combs, scissors and mirrors from a barber-shop to set up business on her own. She knew only a miracle could save her now.

"And I heard of another who was running a forging business. When they broke down the door of his house, they found a copper plate press in a back room, and engraving tools and a drawing for a five pound note of the Bank of Ludlow."

"Oh, the wickedness of that," said a beggarwoman who had never held a five pound note in her life, real or forged.

Annie thought of her father, exiled for passing a forged note, four years before.

"Can people just stop loving other people?" she asked Molly Llewellyn. They were standing in front of the barred window of their cell looking out at the full moon.

"I suppose they can," Molly said, remembering the father of her baby. "Who are you talking about?"

"My father," answered Annie. "You know, he never wrote a single letter to us except the one he sent from the docks in Portsmouth before his ship sailed."

"Maybe he never made it," said Molly, gently. "A lot of people die from the hardships of the voyage, they say. That'll be why he never wrote."

"That's what Mr Evans wanted my mother to think so that she would give in and marry him, but she still loved my father too much. I hope my father is dead, you know, for it would be worse to think he was still out there somewhere but he had just stopped loving us once he arrived on the other side of the world. I hope he is dead, Molly." She sniffed and wiped her nose on her sleeve.

"Shush, Annie, don't say things like that."

"I cannot even remember what he looked like, only that he had a beard, a yellow beard."

"Four years is a long time for you – a third of your life – but he will not have forgotten you. How could he forget his own flesh and blood?" Molly pushed Annie's hair back off her forehead. "Go and lie down, Annie, go and sleep."

Annie looked very poorly, with huge black circles under her eyes, and her skin had become dry and sallow. Her dress, the black work-dress she had been given to wear at Dinham and that had been such a perfect fit, hung on her like a sack, as if she had put on someone else's clothes, someone much taller. Molly wished there was something she could say to comfort her but what was there left to say? The truth was they were both doomed. She looked under her shawl at her own tiny baby, curled up against her like a sleepy kitten. "You will forget me too," she whispered, "for you cannot come with me where I am going."

Across the yard were the men's quarters where William too waited for his trial. The men's cells were as squalid and stinking as the women's but more dangerous places. Fights were common, erupting in sudden unpredictable explosions of violence. William learnt to keep himself to himself, to touch nothing that didn't belong to him and to speak only when a man spoke to him. When they found that he could read and write the prisoners dictated letters to him, pleas to the judge for leniency, last messages to the wives and parents they feared they would never see again. The pennies that he earned from his writing paid the keeper for his rations, for nothing in that hovel came free. They paid for their supper or they did not eat. They coughed up if they wanted a straw mattress to lie on or they slept on the floor awash with filth.

Sam was gone. The day after they had arrived in Shrewsbury, his name had been called out and he was led away. To freedom, William thought, or as much freedom as he could hope for with the drunk useless Israel Bessell for his master. One morning a new prisoner was thrown into the cell. William recognised him as a butcher from Ludlow. He had been arrested for tampering with his weights and measures, filing them down so that he could sell his customers short.

"Sam Price, old Bessell's lad?" he said when William asked him about the little sweep. "Well, they brought him back to Ludlow and put him in the parish workhouse down Old Street for the poor mite had no family to take him in. Old Bessell had disappeared the day after he was let out of the stocks in the square and nobody had set eyes on him again until his body was found floating below the weir at Ludford Bridge. Fell into the river drunk, I expect."

"So Sam is still in the workhouse?" William asked.

"No, no, not at all," said the butcher. "The lad showed a clean pair of heels as soon as they took their eyes off him and ran away again a few days later. That's all I can tell you about Sam, except to say good luck to him for there never was such a lad for smiling in the face of misfortune. He was born a bolter and will stay one as long as he lives."

"He wanted to see the sea," said William, "his heart was set on it."

"We could all be seeing the sea soon enough," said the butcher, "worse luck. May God forgive the man who first

119

thought of banishing Englishmen to Botany Bay," and he spat angrily on the floor of the cell.

The days of the sessions finally arrived. An eerie calm descended on the prisoners, as they contemplated a fate even worse than the one they shared in their cells. One morning they woke to the sound of hammering and knew that the gallows was being erected nearby. The sound affected the men in different ways. A reckless sort of cheerfulness broke out among some of them. "It's the morning drop for all of us," they joked, "the last great leap in the dark." Others threw themselves to their knees and prayed, declaring they would put the wickedness of their lives behind them if only they were spared.

William and Annie saw each other again for the first time in weeks when they were shepherded into the dock on the last morning of the sessions. The court-room was crowded and bewildering. There was a constant to-ing and fro-ing of criminals and nervous witnesses in front of the high bench. A trio of grave stony-faced judges, like balding crows in black gowns and powdered wigs, handed down their judgments. Weasel-faced lawyers came in and out, brandishing long pieces of paper; white-stockinged ushers guarded the doors; clerks at sloping desks wrote furiously, scattering droplets of ink in all directions. Above them all, a sea of spectators looked down from the gallery, like an audience at the theatre who were determined to enjoy the matinee. They passed food to one another, they smoked, they gasped with indignation as the roll call of crimes was read out, they laughed, they were moved to tears.

William and Annie stood, side by side, waiting for their names to be called. From time to time, William reached out and touched Annie's sleeve. A sergeant-at-arms stood beside them, tapping his truncheon in the palm of his left hand.

"William and Anne Spears, formerly of 2, Tanners' Cottages, Lower Corve St., Ludlow, in the County of Shropshire: Anne Spears, you are accused of the theft of silver plate, cutlery, food and other items to the value of five guineas from Dinham House, Ludlow, the property of Lord Powis, at present tenanted by Lucien Bonaparte." The crowd in the gallery drew in their breath at the name of the old enemy and looked down with renewed interest at the children in the dock. "In addition you are accused of absconding when placed under arrest.

"William Spears, you are accused of the theft of two gold sovereigns, the property of Abraham Smart, hatter, of Quality Square, Ludlow and of aiding and abetting Anne Spears in escape. Is there anyone in the court to speak for you?"

Annie looked around, hoping that even at this late stage some miracle would happen, that someone would explain that it had all been a mistake, but no friendly face emerged from the crowd. The judges bent towards one another to confer.

"These are grave offences, hanging offences," said the principal judge at last. The gallery grew still. "All the worse for being carried out by ones so young and so brazen. I am determined to rid this county once and for all of those criminals who would contaminate, if they could, all decent god-fearing working people. They are like bad apples that must be thrown out before their rottenness spreads to the good apples next to them.

"You both, William and Anne Spears, were given every opportunity to improve your station in life with your own labour but you chose to throw those opportunities away, to steal from your employers, to provoke violence, then to run away and evade the law. It is as clear as daylight to me and to any honest citizen that you have inherited your father's wicked character. Furthermore, your cowardly flight from the law has been a great expense upon the public purse. I therefore sentence you, William Spears and Anne Spears, to be taken," (the crowd gasped, anticipating the worst), "taken from here to the port of Portsmouth, and from there to be transported across the seas on the next convict ship bound for Australia, each to remain for seven years."

The hard edges of the court-room dissolved into a haze of moving shapes and figures. Mouths babbled words she could not understand. She could hear the blood roaring in her ears. Her heart was breaking, splintering into a million pieces. Annie looked at William and saw that he was trembling. His face was as white as a sheet but he turned towards her.

"Don't worry, Annie, I will be with you," he said.

Chapter 14

From Shrewsbury, prisoners were taken to the hulks at Portsmouth to wait for the ship that was to carry them into exile. From start to finish the journey was atrocious. They travelled down to the coast in open carts with their legs shackled together and their arms tied. They were given no food or water unless they had money of their own to buy it at the inns where the carts stopped to change their horses. Although it was early June, the weather was cool and at night-time the temperature dropped still further. William and Annie had nothing but the clothes they had been wearing since the day they had fled from Ludlow.

The sad procession made its way through the English country-side, the men in one cart, the women in another. Worst of all was when they had to pass through a village or town, for then the people would come out of their houses to gawp at them and shout good riddance. Annie felt even more ashamed and despised than before and buried her head in her hands so that nobody would see her tears.

123

Molly Llewellyn, who had also been sentenced to transportation, spent the entire journey staring into space. She was dazed with grief and had spoken to nobody since an overseer had come to the prison and taken away her baby son. He was to be put in the parish workhouse at Shrewsbury. Molly knew she would probably never see the child again even if she ever managed to return to England when her four years were up, for she feared the poor mite would soon die of neglect. Another woman on the same cart bought gin at the coaching-house and gave Molly sips of it to deaden her pain.

At Portsmouth, they were herded on to the hulks, the foul rotting battle-ships anchored off-shore that were a temporary prison for the hundreds of ragged and starving-looking convicts waiting to be taken to Australia. If Shrewsbury prison had been bad, life on board the hulks was indescribable. The air below deck was so stale and foul it made you gag. Every square inch of the ship was soaking wet, even the hammocks and bedding, and the whole place was so overcrowded it was like living in a dark unpleasant nest of rats. The sea-water thumped and slapped against the side of the ship. It creaked and groaned and rolled, straining at the rusty anchor. Annie had never seen the sea before – it terrified her, all that grey-green energy heaving and rolling and stretching as far as she could see. When Sam had described it to her, she had imagined it would be as still as a mill pond. The thought of spending six months tossing around on it, beyond all sight of land, made her weak with fear.

A red-headed man with huge calloused hands had set up as a barber, shaving the heads of the newcomers to the hulks. He stood up to his ankles in his clippings, strands and curls of red, brown, black, and blond hair plastered to the wet boards of the deck. Everything about him was brutal. He roughly seized Annie's long blonde hair and chopped it off – she heard later that he kept the longer lengths of women's hair to sell to wigmakers – then clipped the rest almost to the scalp. Smarting with pain and humiliation, she was pushed to the back of another long queue which was shuffling slowly towards a table at the farthest end of the deck where the quartermaster was handing out clothes. Annie had to give up her red cape and received instead the convict's issue, a rough-spun grey striped jacket, a hideous thin petticoat-dress, stockings and a pair of shoes that were far too big. William was heart-broken when they took away his black silk top hat.

"Can I have it back when we dock at Sydney?" he asked.

The quartermaster laughed in his face. "You'll have no call for a hat where you're going, my lad," he said.

After that, they were shackled again, "to stop you thinking of swimming to the shore," the guards told the new arrivals. One of the sailors tied a huge iron ball to Annie's right ankle. It was so heavy, fourteen pounds, and so clumsy that she could hardly walk, but had to drag her leg along the deck, with the iron band biting into her flesh. Grown men, with three times the strength of Annie, had less harsh irons: but they had the money to pay the bribes, and William and Annie had none. There was a black market in everything, and everything had its price, from "easement of irons" to pokes of tobacco, white loaves or shoes that fitted.

Without any money, William thought, as he lay on a stinking hammock that first night and struggled to hold down his nausea, they were as good as dead. He had been warned by other prisoners who had been there longer that the government rations that they were supposed to receive were never enough. Everyone from the captain and his officers to the cook and the Portsmouth tradesmen was on the make. They each took a cut to sell: Annie and William would be lucky to get more than a lump of bread or a maggoty slice of fatty bacon. William's silk hat and Annie's fine red cape were pawned by the quartermaster the very same night.

For three weeks they waited for the transport ship and they worked. Each morning the prisoners were rowed out to the shore to stand in chain gangs and work in the dockyards, breaking up and shovelling coal. They were wet and cold and hungry and always in fear of a flogging. Not a day passed but someone was flogged, tied to the whipping post and beaten almost to the bone, and for no reason other than to keep the whole colony in a state of terror and submission. Proud men and women were reduced to quivering wrecks who dared not look an officer in the eye for fear of giving offence.

At night, in the cover of darkness in their stinking dormitories, Annie and William listened to their companions' stories. Some of these men and women claimed they were innocent of any crimes, some were guilty and repentant; others were plainly evil, and some were just so poor that they had broken laws they could not understand. Hunger had driven a man to dig up cucumbers and cabbages from a kitchen garden on the estate of his landlord. A thirteen-year-old orphan girl had stolen a cloak from a tea-shop. A weaver was accused of organising his work mates into a trade union and "administering illegal oaths". All of these were to be transported under the same rules as a violent slit-throat who had killed three women and left three more for dead.

Right to the last day of these forlorn weeks, there were prisoners who still hoped for a last-minute pardon. They wrote letters (or William wrote for them, earning a few pence or some extra food for his trouble). They urged their families to send petitions to the home secretary, even to the King himself. They begged their local magistrates, or their vicar, sometimes a local duke or landowner, to give them references. Little of this did any good but still the convicts would not give up hope that a word in the right ear or a sum of money placed in the right hand would secure their release. Like drowning men clutching at clumps of seaweed, they held on fast to their conviction that a pardon would come before the ship weighed anchor and sailed out of the harbour.

William wrote too, on his own behalf, not asking for a pardon, but pleading that he and his sister should be allowed to travel together on the same ship and that they should be kept as near as possible to each other on their arrival in Australia. "And," he wrote, "I most humbly and fervently ask if it is possible to have news of the whereabouts of my father, John Spears. We have had no news for over four years. If it is possible, I should like him to know that my sister Annie and I are to be sent shortly to Australia and he should also be told that his wife, Kezia, and youngest daughter Elizabeth, are both dead, perished in a fire at their home in Ludlow in the county of Salop."

When no reply came to this letter, William would not let Annie out of his sight but came, dragging his painful iron ball behind him, to find her every night when he was brought back on to the hulk after his long arduous labour on the docks.

"You must stay near me all the time now, Annie, so that they will not send us on different ships."

Annie's eyes opened wide with horror. "Can they do that? Oh William, I am so afraid. I could not bear the thought of being alone out on the sea."

At last, one morning in June, a rumour spread that a transport ship had already left the docks at London and was expected to arrive at Portsmouth to pick up its final contingent of prisoners. The bay draft, the list of people to be shipped aboard the *Dunlavin*, was read out, one hundred and eighty in all. William and Annie's names were on it. They were going but at least they were going together.

The news that the *Dunlavin* was shortly to sail spread like wildfire. Each morning brought more grief-stricken relatives and friends to the quays to take their last farewells. They stood weeping at the dockside, holding up babies, hollering messages, pleading or bribing the steward to be allowed to board the ship to say a last good-bye. Some had brought tools – axes and hammers for carpenters, anvils for shoemakers, needles, threads, scissors and tapes for seamstresses – hoping one day their relative would be free to earn the passage back to England.

The holds had already been loaded up at the London docks. The ship had to carry enough provisions for the entire journey as well as all the special orders for the colony, which was still a country without shops or factories, where all sorts of goods had to be brought from fifteen thousand miles away. (The first fleet had landed in Australia only twenty-three years earlier in 1788.) There were crates of glassware for the governor's house, bales of woollen cloth and mattress ticking, rolls of carpet, boxes of nails, saws, shovels, hammers, writing paper, an entire blacksmith's forge, cases of Scotch whisky, fishing-line and hooks, four spinning wheels.

Once the Portsmouth batch of convicts were on board, it only remained for the last items of cargo to be laden and the ship would be ready to leave. All day long, the level of noise, the hammering and banging, the slamming of hatches, the barking of orders, drowned out the exiles' farewells. Cattle, crowded into dockside pens, bellowed with anxiety. A tethered ram pawed the ground or smashed his horns against the post where he was tied. Geese corralled into cages hissed and screeched and a pair of Gloucester Old Spots squealed as if their throats were being cut as the sailors hoisted them up on board ship in swaying slings. The stench, already overpowering, grew worse and worse as the frightened animals steamed and sweated in the hot afternoon sun.

The convicts had been put in irons below deck while the ship lay in the dock. Annie and William heard the commotion but saw none of it. Their hearts were sick with loneliness.

Late in the afternoon, a young man and a smaller child pushed their way through the jostling throng, stopped at the foot of the gang-plank and spoke to the armed guards. The older of the two pointed repeatedly at a piece of paper he held in his hand. The child sat down on a stone bollard and watched the sailors climbing the rigging. One of the guards came on board, and approached an officer. He strode off towards the steward's berth. The steward, Thomas Everett, came out on to the deck.

"Midshipman, bring up Annie and William Spears from below," he roared at the sentry.

The prisoners' quarters lay behind a row of iron bars as thick as a man's wrist. One narrow door was set into this, so low and so tight that a stout man could hardly have squeezed through. The berths were in two rows, each of two tiers, each berth "home" for four people for the entire journey though it was hardly six feet square. The air was thick and foul, like the stench of rotten potatoes, for the hatches were kept shut and padlocked even on that summery English day. The guard called out Annie's and William's names.

Dear God, thought William, are we to be freed?

They climbed down to the gangway between the rows of berths, their hearts in their mouths at being singled out like that. Envious eyes watched them as the guard released their irons. Annie and William stole a glance at one another. They could hardly bear to think what might happen to them now and the guard gave no hint as he led them up the steps to Steward Everett's berth.

The door was open. Two figures stood with their backs to them. As the guard pushed William and Annie into the room, the figures turned and there were two faces neither had ever expected to see again: Sam Price and Arthur, the footman from Dinham.

Neither William nor Annie dared move for fear the steward or the guard would lash out at them; both were instantly engulfed by shame on account of their shaved heads and their convicts' uniforms. Arthur and Sam did not hesitate. They wrapped their arms around them both.

"I had to bring you these," said Arthur, handing William a bundle of long slim envelopes all tied up together with an old piece of leather string and smeared with dirt and greasy spots. The top envelope was addressed to Mrs Kezia Spears, in John Spears' large sloping hand-writing.

"What are they, Arthur?" asked William. "How did you come to have them?"

"They are all letters from your father, dating back for years. Leonard Evans gave them to me and told me to make sure you had them before the ship sailed. He was too ashamed to make the journey here himself."

131

"Evans?"

"Yes, it seems he has had them for a long time," Arthur explained. "The top one came on the mail-coach the very day your mother died." He was truly shocked at how poorly the children looked but tried to keep his voice steady. The long months of imprisonment and daily threats of violence seemed to have nearly broken their spirit. "Evans says he didn't want your mother to be upset by them. He thought she should try to forget your father and make a new life for herself."

"Yes, that is true," said William, "for he always used to tell her she would never see our father again."

"The wicked, wicked man," said Sam Price.

"And poor mother never knew he had been writing to her all the time," said Annie, close to tears.

"No," said Arthur, "and then when she died, Evans could not bring himself to admit how he had deceived you all. He hid the letters in a desk and put them out of his mind until a few weeks ago when Abraham Smart came to see him and he confessed what he had done. The hatter did his best, William, pleading with Evans to help get a pardon for you both. He wanted the authorities to let you both work out your sentences here but nobody paid him any heed for, as you know, they all say the poor man is mad. He has taken the whole affair very badly: he never wanted to see your life ruined for the sake of two sovereigns. 'Tell Wills I wish him well', he said, 'I know he never meant to rob me.' "

William took the precious package. There were about half a dozen letters, dating right back to when their father had left for exile. William's head was scrambled with conflicting emotions. He was overjoyed to know that Abraham Smart bore him no ill will, but, more than anything, he was heart-broken. He was overwhelmed by Mr Evans' deceit: he could not bear the thought of poor Kezia dying without knowing that her husband had been writing to her all those years and he was angry to think of his father, all alone in exile, believing that his family had loved him so little they could not be bothered to answer his letters. But he also felt a fool for allowing himself to think he and Annie were about to be freed. Why on earth had he dared hope they were to be plucked from the ship at the last moment? He could not bear the thought of going back down below deck. Arthur put his arm around his shoulder and pulled him towards him.

Annie's cheeks burnt with rage.

"How could that man do such a cruel thing?" she asked. Arthur only shook his head. Sam slipped a hand into hers and squeezed it.

"We are going to sea, too," he said, cheerfully. "Me and Arthur. We're going to India on a merchant ship."

Annie turned to look at Arthur. "You too?" she said.

"Yes, Lucien Bonaparte and his household have recently moved out of Ludlow to live near Worcester. There is no one at Dinham House any longer."

"And did they not ask you to go to Worcester with them?"

"To be honest, Annie, no, they didn't want me and I didn't want to go."

"And how did you find each other?"

"I went to Bristol," Sam said, "like we were trying to do the first time. It took me ages to find the Lamb Inn where Arthur's brother worked. There were sailors lodging there and they got me the job as a cabin boy on their ship."

"And when I lost my job at Ludlow," Arthur interrupted, "I went to Bristol too, hoping David could help me find work with him. And what do you know but Sam was already there, all done up in a sailor suit – I hardly knew him for I had never seen him before with such a clean face."

Sam looked down at his feet, almost embarrassed, and pulled at his trousers.

"That is enough," said the steward, not unkindly. "You will have to leave now. I only let you on because they are so young – the youngest on board the ship."

William, Annie, Sam and Arthur looked at each other, fighting back tears.

"Thank you for coming, Arthur," said William. His voice cracked. "I shall never forget your kindness in bringing us the letters but I am sick and ashamed to let you see us like this."

"It is a bad business, William, but there is no need for you to be ashamed. In Australia, you will find your father, I am sure of it, and God willing, make a life that is fairer to you and your sister than this one in England has been."

"Come along, now," said the steward again. "You have had more than enough time to take your leave."

Arthur put his arms around Annie and William in turn.

"May God bless both of you," he said. Then he and Sam were led away.

The first letter that John Spears had written to his wife was dated nearly four years earlier. William read it out.

". . . after six months at sea, we had our first sighting of the great cliffs and the entrance to Sydney Bay. The harbour itself was empty: not another vessel lay at anchor, but when they caught sight of our sails, every man and woman came down to see the *Julius Caesar* come in to dock, for we were the first ship to come for many months and everyone was eager for letters and news from England. Behind the harbour lies the new town of Sydney, every bit of it from the barracks to the governor's house built by the hands of wretched convicts like myself."

He described how he and his fellow-convicts staggered down the ladder to stand on solid earth again after all the months at sea, many of them sick and feverish or with ulcerous sores from the leg irons they had worn for so long. He said he was working clearing land and trees for building. "The landscape here," he wrote, "is still very strange to me. All around are the tallest trees I have ever seen in my life, gum trees with grey-green patchy bark that we cut down to use for building and fuel. There are giant ferns too and shrubs and grasses, all alien to our eyes, and strange animals and flocks of brightly-coloured birds, yellow and red and pink, flitting and screeching around us, as free to come and go as we are not."

William stopped. He picked up Annie's hand and held it tightly.

"Is there no more?" she asked.

William nodded.

"Then go on," she said. "Read them all."

The last letter ended: ". . . when I think how I have been set down at the edge of this huge empty continent, far from everyone and every place that I love, my heart sinks. At night the endless canopy of sky is filled with stars that you in England have never seen. It is only when I look up at the moon – it is almost full tonight, Kizzy, and hanging so low down over the bay like a huge white lantern that I feel I could stretch out my hand and touch it – it is only when I look up at it that I have the comfort of knowing that you too may be standing under the same moon and thinking of me. Please kiss my little ones, William, Annie and Libby, and know that I am and have always been a loving husband and a dutiful father."

Later that night, Annie woke with a start. Molly Llewellyn, lying next to her, was moaning and sobbing quietly, her body jerking in sleep, reminding Annie of how little Libby used to keep sewing in her sleep though her hands were empty. She reached across and stroked Molly's back until her breathing grew more even. In the berths below and all around her, people snored or coughed or rattled their leg irons as they tried to shift in their sleep, but mostly it was the wind she heard, screaming in the sails, and the cables straining. The *Dunlavin* was bucking like a horse, rocking and rolling, rising and falling in a way she had never known before. It was dark, dark as only a starless night can be out on the open sea. Sometime, while she had been sleeping, the ship had weighed anchor and slipped out of Portsmouth harbour. England already lay behind her, Australia fifteen thousand miles away. She thought of her father, standing there alone under a lantern moon.

Chapter 15

"There is no one of that name listed in the 1811 muster."

The sergeant closed the book.

"But there must be," insisted William. "He has been here for almost five years. S.p.e.a.r.s," he spelt out the name, "John Spears, please look again. Or let me look for myself."

The sergeant was the ugliest man William had ever seen, small, with a barrel-shaped gut hanging out over his trousers, and a fleshy red face which almost covered up his close-set black eyes. He stank of rum. William was not sure the man could read.

He pulled the ledger closer to him so that William could not see the page. "He is not here. There is nobody of that name, I'm telling you."

"Isn't there any other list?"

"This," the officer tapped the book with the point of his pencil, "gives the names and whereabouts of every living soul in all of Australia."

"Did you check Hobart or Norfolk Island? Perhaps he is out on a work-party in the bush? Or with the chain-gangs up in the coal-mines. He could be working for a farmer in the Hunter Valley." William listed off all the places he had heard other transports talking about. "Could he already have come off stores like the man my sister and I work for? He can't just have disappeared."

The sergeant shook his head at every suggestion. He snarled at William through clenched teeth. "Every man, woman and child's name is in the muster book, whether they're still on government stores or taking care of themselves. If he was anywhere in Australia, his name would be here."

"Then where is he?" asked William.

"I couldn't say." The sergeant sucked his teeth. "He could be dead, I suppose, he could have perished from typhus. He could have been murdered. I don't know and I don't care. Maybe he ran away and is living on his wits in the bush. Only Tuesday last a party of surveyors found another skeleton out there, picked clean by those dingo dogs. Maybe that was your father." He spat on the floor, then grinned maliciously at William. His teeth were stained dark black from his chewing tobacco. "On the other hand, he might have got pardoned, I suppose, and gone back to England before he knew his thieving good-for-nothing son was on his way out here too." He cocked his head at William and sneered.

"How can I find out what has become of him? I must know," insisted William.

"What you must know, you impudent rascal, is of no

concern of mine. All I know," he said, standing up and closing the ledger, "is that you're wasting my time here. Forget your father. If he's still alive, and I doubt it, he has probably taken a new wife and has another family of pups to feed. He won't want you turning up out of the blue. Now get out before I have to throw you out."

William fled as the soldier threw a punch at his head and kept running all the way down the long dusty road under the grinding white light of the Australian summer until he reached the cattle yard where Robert Traylor was waiting for him. William had grown taller since he had arrived in New South Wales. His shoulders were broader and he now had feathery blond hair growing on his upper lip and along his arms and legs. He also had a defiant look in his eyes, the look of a young man who has witnessed terrible things but has learned to survive.

He and Annie had finally reached Sydney after one hundred and sixty days at sea. The journey had been unspeakable. Each day for almost half a year, he had seen men at their worst. It was like a secret brutal world where there are no rules. Officers, sailors, and convicts alike all behaved in the most inhuman way. William had seen men flogged so hard their bones had poked through their skinned backs. He had seen the twisted satisfied looks on their torturers' faces as they wielded their whips. Many men and women had died of hunger and disease and neglect. Those who survived grew hard-hearted. Once, a man had told no one that the prisoner in the berth next to him had died so that he could claim the dead man's food rations. It was only when the stink had become unbearable that the truth came out. Everyone, William and Annie too, became infested with body lice which bit and burrowed into their skin day and night so they never had enough sleep. After months of this, it was hard not to think the world was an evil place.

Whatever the weather, the living conditions were awful. Soon after the ship left England, it became cold and wet and they shivered beneath their thin blankets. Later, it was hot and there was no air in the hold for weeks. The ship was becalmed for days with no wind. Later still, after they had left Rio de Janeiro, they met violent storms. For days, the ship rolled and tossed on waves as high as a cathedral steeple. Water poured down on them so that everything on board was soaked through. Lying helplessly below deck locked into their leg chains, William and Annie listened to every ship timber groaning and cracking and the winds screaming.

When the *Dunlavin* finally arrived in Sydney, they were both half-starved to death and so shocked by what they had seen and suffered they were hardly able to say their own names, but they were in luck. Almost immediately they were assigned together to Robert and Peggy Traylor, farmers who had land up along the Parramatta river. William worked with the stockmen, sometimes riding out for days on end with the cattle the Traylors reared and fattened for beef. He grew to love the horses and the heat and the wide open spaces and could hardly believe he had once wanted nothing more than to make top hats. One day when Annie saw him riding into the yard leading a bullock on a rope she realised with a jolt that they were no longer the children they had been in England, and that the life they had led there was gone forever.

Although she was still working as a servant, the Traylors' home could not have been more different from Dinham House. There were no liveried footmen or high-ceilinged salons full of crystal and fine furniture, but a crudely-built wooden farm-house of small hot rooms full of rough men with rougher manners. Annie looked after the three youngest Traylor children, all of them under three years of age, and helped prepare the men's rations but even though it was tough, and the hours were long, Peggy Traylor made a kinder employer than Mrs Stringer from Dinham House. She and William were not slaves, far from it, for the Traylors were kind people and treated them both as well as their own children. They had once been convicts themselves and had suffered cruelly during their early years in Botany Bay. When they had heard about the young brother and sister newly arrived on the transport ship, *Dunlavin*, they had asked to take them in.

Robert Traylor, had been sent out from England on the infamous Second Fleet in 1790 when he was twenty years old.

"Any of us that survived Captain Donald Trail can survive anything," he told William. Of the four hundred and ninety nine convicts who had set out on the *Neptune*, one hundred and fifty eight had died on the voyage; only a handful of those who disembarked were fit enough to begin work. It had the most calamitous record of all the convict ships that ever sailed from England.

During the seven years of his sentence, Robert had tried to escape twice. The first time he had headed inland into the bush but after two weeks wandering around dazed with heatstroke and hunger, had come back into Sydney and given himself up. He was given one hundred lashes with the cat o' nine tails and sent to Norfolk Island, a settlement several thousand miles off the coast, where he and four others had almost immediately begun to build a raft, with the hope of reaching China. That escape ended in disaster too when they were washed up on a small coral island where an East Indies trader picked them up and brought them back to Sydney.

When the long hard seven years of his sentence were finally up, he had stayed on, reckoning he could make a better go of things in Australia than in his native Sussex. He had been one of that first generation of convicts to come off government stores, one of the first men to be given a grant of land, the tools to clear it, and convict labour to help him work it. It was only thirty raw acres of bush to begin with, but by the time the Spears were sent to work for him he had more than three hundred acres along the Parramatta river. He had done well, raising cattle for beef which he sold back to the government.

Peggy Traylor, Robert's wife, was an Irishwoman who ruled her home and her farm with an iron fist. She could fell trees, build fences, dig drains, ride a horse, take hold of a tangled-up calf and pull it out from its mother, and lower a pint of rum as well as any man. She was as big and broad as the blacksmith who called on Saturdays to shoe the horses.

At weekends her house was full of loud Irishmen, singing ballads into the small hours or holding arm-wrestling competitions at the kitchen table. The floorboards trembled as Peggy pushed and shoved people around the room, shouting out instructions for the ceili dancing at the top of her voice. She was a "political", transported for her part in the failed rebellion in Ireland in '98.

"I'll help youse find your father," she told Annie and William when they told her the story of how Leonard Evans had deceived them and kept their father's letters. "God bless him, he must be terrible anxious with no news from you all these years."

It had been her idea to see if John Spears' name appeared on the muster which had been taken the previous year.

"Wouldn't it be a fine thing if you could all be together again after all the hardships you've been through? There's worse places than Australia, you know, though I'm sure you didn't think that when you were standing in the dock back in England."

"Don't you miss your home in Ireland?" asked Annie.

"Oh, I do indeed, darling. I miss my people but sure I have Robert here now and the children. There's relations of mine back in Wexford that would have forty fits if they knew I had gone and married an Englishman! And, to tell you the god honest truth," she lowered her voice, "I'm a million times better off here than ever I could have been in Wexford. I'm not denying the early years were a terrible hardship, but there's a future to be had here, for you and your brother too."

"I don't miss England," said Annie, "for there is no one there for us any more. I like it better here with you – but I wish we were able to find out where our father was."

"You and your brother will always have a home here with us, Annie, even if you don't find your own father. Now would you put on a couple of eggs to boil for the children's supper? I'd better get back to my digging though I doubt if anything we sow this year will grow unless the rains come soon."

Peggy Traylor was as good as her word. When Robert said he was taking the cattle down to sell at Sydney market and bring back new stock, Peggy insisted that William should ride along with him and go and check the muster list. They had been away for days and Annie was hardly able to sit still for five minutes at a stretch with the excitement as she waited for them to return.

It was late at night when the stockmen got back to the farm on the banks of the Parramatta river. Annie had woken up when she heard the horses out the back and the racket coming from the kitchen where Peggy was putting out food and drink for the exhausted drovers. She got out of bed and went out to look for her brother.

She found him sitting on the stoup outside, watching the reflection of the full moon gliding over the surface of the river. Even in the early hours of the morning it was hot. The air was heavy with the smell of eucalyptus. Cicadas croaked. It was enough to see his slouched shoulders and the exhausted look on his face to know the news was bad. He looked up as she sat down beside him.

"I'm sorry, Annie," he said. "No luck."

In the corral behind the farm-house the horses were restless. They whinnied and raced round in circles. Flickering shadows moved behind the gum trees. The earth which had been baked dry for months was like a piece of skin stretched to tearing point. A lizard had clamped itself against the step of the veranda next to William but scuttled away over the carpet of brittle fallen leaves when Peggy Traylor came out from the house.

"Robert tells me your father's name was not on the muster, William," she said.

"No," said William. "The officer said there is no one in the whole country with the name of Spears."

"Arrah, you wouldn't believe that. There are hundreds of people not on any of their old lists. They might have spelt his name wrong. He'll show up one of these days, take my word for it."

William shook his head. "I don't know any more, Mrs Traylor. I feel like giving up."

Peggy put her hands on her hips and glared at him.

"What sort of talk is that? That's what the System wants you to do, wanted all of us to do, just shut up and ask for nothing. You have every right to know what has become of your father. And he has every right to know what has become of you."

Annie nodded enthusiastically. "Mrs Traylor is right, William. We must not give up until we find him."

A loud explosion of laughter came from the kitchen.

"Have you talked to the drovers to see if any of them ever came across him?" asked Peggy.

"Of course," said Annie, "and it is always the same. Nobody has ever heard of him."

"Now, darling dear, don't give up hope. People are always being moved around from one settlement to another. That way they think the men will have no time to hatch plots and set up a rebellion against the whole stinking system. Sure, I was never more than a couple of months in the one place myself until I got my ticket-of-leave and came out here to Parramatta with the bould Robert. I suppose they thought an Irishwoman like me would contaminate all around me with my opinions."

There was a shuffling noise from under the veranda.

"What is that?" said Annie, as an awkward-looking beast blundered into view. It was like a small bear and yet quite unlike a bear, with a blunt snout and short thick legs. The land was full of strange wild beasts, weirder than anything ever dreamt of in England. Every day huge flocks of kangaroos bounded across the dry brush. Only the day before, down by the river, she had seen a creature that looked as if it was made up of parts of a whole lot of other animals for it had a furry body but a beak for a mouth and feet like a duck. It laid eggs, but then suckled its young! And now here was something else just as odd.

Peggy smiled at Annie's startled face. "Have you never seen a wombat? They tunnel around under the ground. God only knows why it's on the move at this time of the night. And the horses are very restless too. Maybe it's just this terrible heat getting to them." She stood up and stretched. "Now come in inside and get a bite to eat, William, for you must be starving. One of the new cattlemen might know something about your father. Annie, you come along too."

The cattle drovers were gathered in a circle around the kitchen table, playing cards. Nobody looked up as they came in. There was a vague smell of poteen, the hooch that Peggy made with maize, and the air was almost blue with the smoke from the men's pipes.

Robert Traylor, seated at the top end of the table, was half the size of his wife but there was not a man in New South Wales who would have made a joke about it. Robert was small but tough and could lay a man out flat on the ground if he had a mind to. As he said himself, after his experiences on the voyage from England under the notorious villain, Donald Trail, he could fight his own corner. He was a fairly rich man now, with many men working for him, but he still preferred to sit in his kitchen with his assigned convict workers rather than lord it in a parlour full of imported carpets and over-stuffed arm-chairs.

As the door opened and Peggy led William and Annie in, he looked up from his hand of cards.

"I'm just getting a bit of grub for William," Peggy explained.

"Come in, come in," said Robert, "pull up a couple of chairs. I expect you're very disappointed, Annie, that William had no luck in Sydney."

Annie nodded.

"It's a rum business, to be sure, but those lists are only as good as the men who make them. We'll find him, wherever he is."

Peggy turned around from the range.

"Did any of youse men ever run into a John Spears from England?" she asked the card-players. "He's the father of these young ones."

"What's he doing out here?" one of the men grunted, throwing his cards face-down on the table.

"They said he passed a forged note," said William.

"Forgery? Good on him, mate," said one of the other men as he shuffled the cards and dealt out the pack again.

"Have you heard of him? He's been here for about five years. John Spears." Peggy repeated.

"No, I don't remember ever coming across a forger," said the first man.

"He was a tanner, from Shropshire," Annie said. Both she and William had long since stopped telling people their father was innocent. Innocent or guilty, all the transports had suffered the same. "He used to have a blond beard."

"If he was Irish, I might have heard of him," said another, swallowing the last mouthful of the poteen in his glass and wiping his mouth with the back of his hand, "but, in any case, if he's been here as long as you say, he could well have got his ticket-of-leave, and will be working for himself. I hear there's men heading further west and north now, taking up new grants of land." He pushed himself back from the table and balanced his chair on its back two legs, studying his hand of cards.

"I saw men and waggons this morning," said Robert, "driving sheep up the valley. I reckon they had a couple of hundred ewes at the very least." He abruptly rose from the table, walked over to the open window and sniffed the hot air. The horses were still nervously circling the corral.

"They seem edgy tonight, Peg," he said, "Did you see anybody out there? Anyone moving about? Bushrangers?"

"No more shadows than any other night," his wife replied, "but something is up with the poor beasts to be sure. C'mon out a minute, all of ye."

Peggy led the four men outside. William and Annie followed behind. A new noise had started up, like the sound you heard if you picked up one of the enormous conches on the beach and put it to your ear, William thought, though it was magnified a thousand times greater than that. It was the sound of air rushing, a hot high wind fanning the whole continent.

"There's the trouble," shouted Peggy, suddenly pointing towards a distant red glow up on the ridge above the valley. "May God protect us. That's the last thing we needed."

"What is it?" asked Annie.

"The bush is on fire," said Robert Traylor, grimly, "and it's blowing this way. We'll need to move fast if we're to save the farm and the dwelling. Those blazes travel like the devil." The farmer's voice was quite steady but William could sense the anxiety welling up from his stomach. Even in the few months he had been with the Traylors, William had heard stories about bushfires, about how they engulfed everything in their path, advancing like a wall of death across the landscape, devouring trees, scrub, fences, bridges, buildings, farm animals. They could rage for days, reducing areas hundreds of miles across to a parched black lifeless desert, undoing the efforts of years and years.

Even before her husband had finished speaking, Peggy was racing back towards the house to fetch her children.

"Get up, get up," she was shouting. "There's a fire up on the ridge."

Men began to come running out of the long hut where they slept, pulling on their shirts, asking what needed to be done.

"Which way is it travelling?"

"Is there a break between it and us?"

"For God's sake, will someone do something to calm those horses!"

In the dark heat of the night, all peace was shattered.

William glanced at Annie. She had turned completely pale and was staring with wide panicky eyes at the distant wall of fire up on the hills.

"Oh William," she murmured. "Not a fire, not here too."

She had a sudden heart-breaking flashback of the burnt-out shell of the house where her mother and sister had perished and the hump of red earth on the grave where they lay far away in Ludlow. She remembered too that other night when she had looked down on the blazing effigy of Napoleon and the hate-filled faces outside Dinham House. Had she and William survived all they had been through only to lose their lives in another fire?

Standing in the coppery moonlight, Annie could see a curtain of hot air shimmering a long way off. The heat dissolved everything, turning solid rock to fluid insubstantial waves of light. The high dry wind fanned the fire, coaxing it down the valley. Even in the short time she had been watching, she could see it had drawn nearer, growing larger all the time as the flames spread from treetop to treetop. The sky on the horizon blazed red and gold. Clouds of birds flapped urgently overhead; a herd of kangaroos fled past, their stamping feet sending vibrations through the earth like tribal drums.

Suddenly, Peggy Traylor thrust a screaming baby into Annie's arms.

"Come on," she said, dragging her away by the elbow, "you take Seanie. I'll carry the other two. We've got to get you all across the river."

Years before when Robert Traylor had been given his first grant of land on the Parramatta, he and his work-gangs had cleared a broad strip either side of the bank and dug the ashes of the timber into the soil as a fertiliser. Now that narrow strip along the river was their only chance of halting the fire in its trail of destruction, a natural break which the raging cliff of fire could not cross.

Annie ran after the fleeing figures. Looming over her, drovers on horseback whooped and yelled as they drove their precious cattle down to the bank, breaking and trampling underfoot the tall stems of maize that were almost ready for harvesting. The river was deep and wide where it flowed through the Traylor land, so wide and so deep it made the rivers Teme and Corve of Ludlow seem no more than creeks. This was not a place any man would have chosen to cross with three hundred head of cattle, fifteen horses and all the members of his household but there was no alternative. The panicky beasts bellowed and tried to climb over one another as the men steered them towards the black water.

Annie looked back over her shoulder. The fire was getting even closer. The smell of smoke caught her throat. The air was thick with tiny smuts of soot like flying insects which clung to her skin as she ran through them. The baby she was carrying coughed and sobbed but Annie just clutched him even tighter to her breast and ran on. She had lost sight of Peggy and of William. All along the river bank, men were screaming, hitting the water with long sticks, driving the wild-eyed terrified animals forward.

A couple of hundred yards down river from them, the party that Robert Traylor had seen that morning trekking up the valley were busy rounding up their ewes. Two tense collie dogs crouched low on the ground, their ears alert for every command, every whistle. The sheep bunched together until they were cornered in between the riverbank and the waggons pulled up behind. One of the trekkers had dragged a long sheet of wood down from one of the waggons and slipped it into the river. As Annie drew nearer, she saw Peggy handing him the two tiny bundles that were the other Traylor children.

"Wait for us," she screamed, running awkwardly across the dry uneven ground with the baby bouncing painfully against her, but the man had already pushed off from the bank. He was standing up, steering his makeshift raft with a long pole. The raft bounced and rolled and drifted downstream. Annie reached the bank and stood beside Peggy, who took the baby from her arms and put a hand around her shoulder.

"You go across next with little Seanie," the Irishwoman said to her.

"Will you not come with us too?" asked Annie. She could not bear the thought that she would be all alone again in the world if anything happened to Peggy Traylor.

"Not yet, darling. I'll go back and help the men with the animals once I know all you children are safe. Don't worry about me. Just keep an eye on my babies for me and I'll be with you as soon as I can."

They watched the raft's uncertain path until it finally reached the opposite bank and the ferryman lifted the children on to dry land.

"Thanks be to God for that man, whoever he is," Peggy murmured.

Later, John and Annie Spears would compete to tell the end of the story. He said he had felt the first drop of rain fall upon his cheek as he pushed the raft off from the bank on its return journey. He looked up at the sky and the high black clouds gathering behind the full moon.

"Alleluia, thank God for rain," he thought, rowing hard for the shore where a small girl with a halo of gold hair had joined the mother of the children he had just set down. As he drew closer, he fancied for a moment he had seen her before although he had only come up the Parramatta valley that day on his way west to the land he had been granted.

Kezia, he thought, she has the look of Kezia about her, and felt once more the pang of heart-break that the wife he loved so much and had had to leave behind in England had never once replied to his letters.

Annie watched the man rowing furiously towards the bank. There was something familiar about him, she thought, something that made her feel briefly happy and unafraid. Behind her, she heard a roar go up from the stockmen as the clouds burst and the rain began to fall, huge warm drops rolling down her cheeks like tears. The river danced. The ground steamed and a thousand frogs suddenly broke into defiant chorus. William raced past her, shouting, "Annie, Annie, come on."

Down at the river edge, some of the waggoners had knelt down to steady the raft as the man who had punted the Traylor children to safety reached the bank. One of them held out his shepherd's crook and the man seized it and leapt on to the bank.

Over the chaotic croaking of the frogs, the bellowing of the cattle, and the bleating of bewildered sheep, Annie could hear the man with the blond beard shouting, "Annie! William!"

And as her brother flew into the man's open arms, Annie knew she was finally surfacing from a nightmare that had gone on far too long. She hurtled towards her father, with warm rain-drops coursing down her face. The moon hung overhead like a lantern behind a veil of rain.

Look for other BEACON BOOKS
published by Poolbeg

*"Literary books for discriminating
young adult readers"*

∾

The Song of the River by Soinbhe Lally

Charlie's Story by Maeve Friel

Circling the Triangle by Margrit Cruickshank

The Homesick Garden by Kate Cruise O'Brien

When Stars Stop Spinning by Jane Mitchell

Shadow Boxer by Chris Lynch

Different Lives by Jane Mitchell

Ecstasy and other stories by Ré Ó Laighléis

∾

BEACON BOOKS